Jax & Marbles

Jax & Marbles

JACQUELINE LORRAINE CONWELL

authorHOUSE®

AuthorHouse™
1663 Liberty Drive
Bloomington, IN 47403
www.authorhouse.com
Phone: 1-800-839-8640

Published by AuthorHouse   08/13/2012

ISBN: 978-1-4772-5996-2 (sc)
ISBN: 978-1-4772-5995-5 (hc)
ISBN: 978-1-4772-5970-2 (e)

Library of Congress Control Number: 2012914567

For once you are going to hear a dream that I have made sound . . . I dreamt all this: never could my poor head have invented such a thing purposely.
—Richard Wagner, *"Tristan und Isolde"*

Dedicated to my family and friends. Thank you for believing in me and my writing all these years.

Prologue

For nights I looked up into the starry sky and wondered, w*hy?* Why I wondered "why" was always beyond me. The more I tried to figure out "why," the further the thought took me into the humid, royal-blue nightscape as I sat at the window in my room. I hated the feeling of being alone, feeling as though the world was tugging, pulling, and gnawing at my stomach before I went to sleep every night. It felt as though something was missing inside me, but what it was, I could never put my finger on. There was always the hope that someone or something bigger than me in the grand scheme of things would answer me one day. Said someone or something always seemed a little too busy to take note of the words I spoke every night. But that never stopped me from leaving messages before I closed my eyes for the day or from wishing on the diamond-like stars that soared across the sky.

"All I want is for this void to be filled by a *real* friend, someone who won't ditch me when other people come into the picture. Maybe then I wouldn't feel like a piece of me was missing. I'll continue to be patient until things change, I guess. I'm tired of feeling as if I'll be a loner the rest of my life."

After propping myself on the window sill to stargaze a while longer, I felt something other than my own hand touch the side of my face. For a brief moment, the overall feeling of being alone disappeared, and the empty void was full. What filled it, I wasn't too sure of. As I wondered *what* it could have been, I also wondered *who*. Who could have looked down on me and been able to take away that overwhelming loneliness momentarily?

I sat up and stared at a single star that was shining brighter than the rest, wondering if it was just me or if something out of the ordinary had just happened. I blamed it on my overactive imagination as I sighed in frustration, letting questions swirl around in my mind again. If something was going to happen to change the way things were going for me, *why* couldn't it happen now? *What* had made me this way to begin with—depending on wishes, unheard prayers, and unanswered questions? *When* would I feel whole again?

The biggest question I always ended up asking at the end of the day was, *why me?*

Chapter 1

My arrival to this world was unexpected, but it must have happened for a reason. *Everything* happens for a reason. I remember it like it was yesterday . . .

I was on my way home from a local bookstore, where I had just purchased school supplies for my freshman semester at the local community college. I didn't live far from the store, so I'd decided to walk there since the weather was nice. I was only a block or two away from home, when I heard a bunch of people screaming. I remember hearing a few pops behind me and then feeling something hot and sharp hit the back of my neck.

Then everything went black.

When I woke up, I found myself in a large, cold, lime-green-tinted room. There were two or three silver tables in the center with white cloths draped over them. Next to the tables were trays of stainless steel tools that were shining brightly under the ceiling lights. I was confused as to where I was, until I looked down at the table closest to me and saw *my* body lying on it. Gauze was wrapped around my neck with a dry circle of blood right in the center. That was when I realized I was in a morgue.

I remember trying to suppress the growing panic attack as I touched my cold, clammy body lying on the table. I almost ran out through the morgue doors, but I felt something tug on the bottom of my shirt before I could even take my first step. Standing next to me was a little girl with big, sparkling eyes, wearing all white. There was a pureness to her that made some of the panic forming in my stomach pass. I asked her what she was doing there, and she gave me a huge smile as a set of doors appeared opposite the ones I had been ready to run through.

"I'm here to help you, Jax." She took a hold of my hand gently.

For a brief moment I hesitated.

"Don't be afraid; everything will be okay. Follow me."

And that's how I arrived here.

It was the way I'd imagined it would be when I passed on to the new world I now called "home." Movies and TV shows I'd used to watch had always made the afterlife out to be a journey to large, golden gates where you would check in and play instruments or eat fruit—or both—while coasting around on clouds. I believed *my* afterlife would be spent the way *I* wanted it to be spent: in a large house in the middle of an emerald-green field of tall grass surrounded by large willow trees. There would be a distant pond with water as clear as glass and a vast flower garden with a small shed off to the side. My thing was: if I had to spend an eternity somewhere when I died, why not end up in an environment that'd be to my liking? I think it was because of that logic that I got exactly what I wanted.

For the most part, I was content with my new living arrangement. The only drawback was that I had to stay in my slice of paradise alone. On many nights I would ask for company, but later I would wake up and find an item instead—one that I wanted but that I'd tried to keep in the back of my mind. No matter how many times I tried, I always got the opposite of what I was really yearning for. I was always grateful for the items, so I kept telling myself that with patience I just might get what it was I really wanted.

On a daily basis, I checked in on my parents via a small portable TV I'd received a few days after I arrived. I vowed to check on them every day until I knew they were finished grieving. As I got comfortable under one of my favorite willow trees, I watched my father find what seemed to be an empty sneaker box on a far-right shelf of the closet in my bedroom.

When he opened it, he found a picture of the both of us sitting at the kitchen table from when I was younger. He had been watching me color my nickname, Jax, onto a piece of construction paper. It was one of the first words I was able to spell and write on my own. My real name was Julian, but as I got older, my friends started calling me Jules, while my entire family called me Jax. My father said I got that nickname because it was my favorite game to play with him when I was old enough to understand how it was played. Every time he told me how I got the nickname, we would play a few rounds on the kitchen floor.

I watched as my father kissed the picture, folded it, and tucked it into his back pocket as he walked out.

Sometimes I watched them tidy up my old room a little, but they never made my bed, washed my dirty clothes, or disturbed items of clothing in my closet. I guessed that they wanted to keep a piece of me there for as long as they could.

I yawned lazily as I switched off the portable TV, set it next to me in the grass, and watched the clouds slowly float by in the pale-blue sky. I rested my back against the tree trunk and listened to the breeze blow through the branches. It felt as if something out-of-the-norm would happen that day, but I didn't pay that feeling any mind. Instead, I thought about a handheld gaming system and a random racing game I wanted to play. It appeared before my eyes in less than a second. I grabbed it out of the air, loaded the game, and switched on the power to begin playing.

I had only made it to the second level of the game, when I felt like I was being watched.

"Julian," I heard from one of the branches above me.

I turned off the game and set it next to the portable TV as I slowly rose to my feet. I looked around, but no one was there—at least to the naked eye.

"Hey, G," I greeted with a smile as I felt a light breeze swirl around me.

"How is your day going so far?"

"It's going okay. I have no complaints."

I watched as a large white orb slowly started to appear out of thin air. As it floated away from the tree, I walked alongside it in the same direction it was heading. I never knew the *true* form or even the gender of the deity, and I never asked. G was whatever *I* imagined, and that was all that mattered to me.

We approached a large pond a few yards away from the front of the house, located in the middle of a willow tree grove. I jumped onto a large rock and sat with my legs hanging over the edge. My right sneaker had managed to become untied on the way there, so the tips of the shoelaces rested in the water; disturbing the stillness of the surface.

"Is everything okay with the house?" G asked, hovering close by my side.

"Yes, everything is good. Thanks for asking." I said as I tied my sneaker before the shoelaces got too wet.

"And how are your parents?"

"Today my dad found a picture of us from when I was a kid. My mom is doing okay. They're still grieving and everything, but they're getting by."

We both remained silent for a few seconds, and I watched as the tree branches seemed to dance with the grass in the breeze.

"I am actually here to discuss something with you, Julian."

I picked up a smooth rock and threw it into the pond, watching it as it skipped all the way to the other side. "It's about what I've been asking for, isn't it?"

The orb left my side and positioned itself in front of me. "Yes. I have noticed that you still ask for the same thing every other night. Are you not happy with what you have and what you are able to receive?"

"I am. I'm *very* grateful; don't get me wrong. And I take care of everything I get. I'm lonely, that's all." I placed my chin in my hand, resting my elbow on my left knee while lazily swinging my legs. "I just wish I could have some company."

G quietly processed what I'd said for a moment. "I want to show you something. Follow me."

Before I could ask any questions, the orb whizzed off, quickly making its way around the pond to the other side.

"Wait! Slow down!"

I jumped to my feet and tried to keep up the best I could, following the trail of parted grass in front of me. After another moment of running, I found myself on the other side of the pond. G was waiting at the edge.

"Look here in the water."

I walked over and watched as the surface began to shimmer. An image slowly appeared as I got down on my hands and knees. Patiently I waited for it to be clear enough to decipher what it was. When it finally cleared up, I could see everything as if I was looking through a window.

"It's a girl," I said in disbelief. She was in her bedroom, gazing at the stars through a large window as she sat at the foot of her bed. When I looked closer, I noticed that she was talking. "I can't hear her." I looked to the orb and watched as the white light it emitted slowly began to get brighter. Seconds later, I was able to hear what she was saying.

"All I want is for this void to be filled by a *real* friend, someone who won't ditch me when other people come into the picture. Maybe then I wouldn't feel like a piece of me is missing. I'll continue to be patient until things change, I guess. I'm tired of feeling as if I'll be a loner the rest of my life."

When she finished speaking, she rested her chin in her left hand and propped herself on the windowsill, and continued to stargaze.

I looked over a few of the items in her room. "She seems like she should have a pretty active social life," I said. "It doesn't make sense that she feels like a loner. She *certainly* doesn't look like one." I took note of the books she had on her desk and discovered that she was a freshman in college. She also had a few random figurines of characters from movies that she obviously enjoyed, along with a few video games. Clothes scattered around her room showed that she was a casual but trendy dresser.

"Her name is Alexia. She feels lonely, just like you. The difference between you two is that she is still alive."

I looked back at Alexia and stuck my hand in the water to touch her right cheek. She sat up slowly and put her hand on the area I'd touched, as the image began to fade away. Seconds later, all I could see was my own reflection again.

I scooted away from the pond, sat Indian-style on a patch of moss, and stared into the water blankly, playing back what she'd said in my mind. *No one should feel that way*, I thought.

"What can I do to help?"

"I am glad you asked." G began to float away slowly. I rose to my feet and listened intently to the proposition presented to me as we left the pond. By the time we got back to the house, G had filled me in on everything, and I had a decision to make.

"So, I can go back to the world of the living?" I sat under the tree G had found me under earlier that day and rested my back against it.

"Yes. Of course, there are the terms and conditions I described, and if you find they do not suit you, you do not have to go through with this. If I did not think you would be interested or could not handle the task, I would not have approached you with it. Do you think this is something you will want to do? Once everything is in motion and things finalize, there is no turning back until I call you home for the last time. If you need time to think about it, I understand."

If I go back, I'll be able to live the way I was meant to, I thought. *But I'll have to live in a completely different state from my old home. I also won't be able to check on my family and friends anymore. Do I really want to give that up?* That was the part of the agreement I wasn't too keen about.

But then I thought about Alexia. She needed someone, and that wasn't something I could ignore.

In order for me to be able to go back and stay until it's time for me to come back here, I'll have to gain her trust so she'll accept me as someone she can confide in. Can I really pull that off?

Deep in my heart of hearts, I knew what I had to do—that it was something I *could* do. It would benefit me. It would benefit Alexia. And if my parents could have seen what I was about to do, I knew they would've been so proud.

"I'll do it."

Chapter 2

I started to prepare for my descent back to the world of the living. There wasn't much to do, really, other than to mentally prepare. I had been dead for over a year and had gotten pretty used to my new daily routine. To go back and actually be able to interact with people without being socially awkward was something I was a little worried about. I needed to blend in to the new place I'd be calling home, so I wouldn't stick out like a sore thumb. Alexia couldn't know about what had happened to me, or it'd compromise everything. If *that* happened, I'd have to come back sooner than planned, and I'd lose my second chance at life. I wanted to do everything in my power to make sure my cover wouldn't be blown.

G informed me that I'd meet others like me who would help make the transition back into that world easier. Knowing that I wouldn't be alone every step of the way made me feel more at ease. They were going to do everything they could to help me keep my true purpose and origin under wraps. That included providing me with a place to stay, a car to drive, a job at some point . . . things of that nature, which sounded simple enough on their part. Someone had been notified in advance that I'd be arriving that night and had agreed to touch base with me at a mutually acceptable meeting place. I was worried that I'd screw up royally.

"You will be fine," G assured me. "The first few days may be a little rough, but you will get through it, and it will be as if you had never skipped a beat."

"I've been trying to tell myself that."

"I know you are nervous, but that will pass. I want this transition to go as smoothly as it possibly can. That is why I found someone to help you for the first few days—or weeks, if you need more time to adjust. Remember, you will need to conduct yourself in the same manner you would have if you were back in your home state and had not passed away. You will have your setbacks, of course, but you and I both know that is a part of life."

"What about my name? Will that need to change?"

"Not at all. Just make sure nobody catches on to the fact that something happened to you a year ago and that you are *not* supposed to be there."

"I can do that," I chirped.

"Good. Continue preparing for your departure. I will send for you when it is time to go."

When I felt that I had mentally prepared enough, I headed out to sit under my favorite tree to relax until it was time to leave. After changing into a different set of clothes, I walked out of the house, gently closing the door behind me. As I walked away from it, I felt a cool breeze swirl around me. I looked back, and watched as the house began to fade away, along with the flower garden and the small wooden shed. I stared in awe until there was nothing left but green grass swaying in the breeze as the sky began to turn cotton-candy pink and orange. When the sun began to set, that's when it hit me. *This is really happening. Once I leave, everything here will disappear until the day I come back.*

I turned to make my way to the tree again and bumped into someone standing behind me.

"Are you ready to go, Jax?"

I looked down to find the same little girl who had brought me there a year ago. Her eyes twinkled as she waited for me to respond.

"Is it time already?"

"Yes. Come with me."

She took my hand and led me away from the empty spot where the house had been. As we approached the pond and willow tree grove, they slowly began to fade away as well. After a few moments, there was nothing left but the same tall grass that had remained after the house and everything around it had disappeared. We walked for a few more minutes to the very edge of the area that I was living in. I had never been so far away from the house before, so I was taken aback. It was a little intimidating to look down and see nothing but swirling clouds and darkness. Seconds later, everything calmed and the clouds parted, showing what looked to be a path made of stars.

"Thank you." I squeezed the little girl's hand, and she squeezed mine back just as hard.

"Wait here. G will see you off." She let go of my hand and skipped off in the direction we'd come from. Once she was out of sight, G appeared by my side. The orb hovered closely in silence as I stared at the path before me.

"If you need to rethink this, please do not hesitate to ask for more time," G offered.

"No, I want to do this. I'm ready."

"Okay. Take this path. It will lead you down to a public park. Wait there patiently. When your contact arrives, he will take you to where you will be staying. Good luck. And remember: no matter where you are, I will always be with you."

I took a deep breath and readied myself for what looked to be a long walk ahead of me. "Thanks for this opportunity. I appreciate it more than you know. I'll fulfill my end of the agreement. You have my word."

"I know you will, Julian."

I eyed the starry path curiously, worried I'd fall through if I put all my weight on it. Lightly placing my right foot on it first to test it, I was surprised to find that it was solid, despite its appearance. I placed my left foot on it to be sure and then proceeded forward at a steady pace.

~

After taking a few steps, I found myself walking through a dimly lit park. I stopped for a second and looked around. Fireflies were flashing in the bushes and trees, while crickets were making music in a distant playground section.

"Wow," I whispered in awe as I made my way to the first bench I saw. No one was around, so I took a seat on the moist wood, slouching as I got comfortable. A star twinkled brightly above me from what seemed to be the same direction I'd come from. I smiled, and the star dimmed a little to look like the others around it.

"Hey!"

I jumped when someone greeted me from behind the bench and hopped over the back of it to sit next to me. Once the stranger was comfortable, he looked up at the sky the same way I had done before he'd startled me.

"Hey," I responded. I wasn't sure how I'd know if people who approached me were regular people or the contacts who knew about me. I didn't want to blow it my first night back, so I played it cool.

"Waiting for someone?" he asked.

"Maybe . . ."

"What's your name, friend?"

"Julian."

"Nice to meet you, Julian. I'm James." He extended his hand and waited for me to place mine in it. I complied, shaking it firmly to match his grip.

"So, I'll ask you again, Julian: you waiting for someone?"

I hesitated. "Y-yes. I haven't been waiting for too long, so I'm sure they'll arrive shortly."

"Well, you're in luck." He laughed. "I'm the person you're waiting for. I'm here to take you to your new place and get you settled in. You ready?"

I felt a wave of relief when he confirmed that he was my contact. He didn't look much older than I did; if anything, he was probably the same age. I had kind of expected to meet up with an elderly gentleman, but I was happy with the person I got.

"Yeah, sure. I'm ready when you are."

Just as we were about to leave, we both froze in our tracks when we heard a low growl. He looked at me, stared for a second, and then began laughing loudly. That was when I realized that it was my stomach. I was hungry—a feeling I hadn't experienced in *so* long that I'd forgotten what it felt and sounded like. I tried not to feel so overwhelmed.

"That's embarrassing," I chuckled.

"We'll take care of that on the way."

He placed his hand on my shoulder and guided me to a nearby parking lot, where we hopped into his car and drove into the night. We stopped at a local burger joint and picked up a bag of food and some soda. I ate slowly, as he filled me in on everything I'd have to get adjusted to. I was trying to listen to him so I didn't miss anything, but I was enjoying the taste of food again so much, that I found myself zoning out as I savored every bite and sip I was taking.

Before long we were standing in a gated complex for what looked to be luxury apartment homes. He was giving me a chance to look at the car he'd parked next to, before we headed up to my unit. Apparently it was the one I'd been promised so I could get around town.

"I was told you were good with stick shift," James commented as I walked around the car, peeking through the windows. "I hope that was accurate."

"Yes, it's perfect. It's like what I drove back home."

"I know it's not new or anything, but it's not a clunker, either. I've secured a screwdriver under the front bumper and put additional tools and things in the trunk for emergencies."

He gave me the car keys and a small wallet. Upon opening it, I found a driver's license inside. The address on it looked to be the place where I would be staying, and whoever had made it had somehow found a way to get an accurate picture of me for the photo section. He then handed me the key to my unit and led me up the stairs so we could check out my new place.

We got to the second floor and entered a decent-sized, one bedroom/one bath, furnished apartment. He gave me a brief walk around to show me the location of my bedroom, the bathroom, and all the important light switches. I had a fridge full of food and a TV to watch, and in the dresser drawers I found clothes that looked like they were my style and size. Fresh towels were folded in the linen closet, and extras were in the small laundry room that had a full-sized washer and dryer inside. After the tour, he told me he had to go, but he'd see me the next day.

"You've got a big day ahead of you tomorrow. You'll start tagging along with me so you can learn your way around town. It may take a few days, but I'm sure you'll catch on fast."

I walked him to the door, and he stepped out into the breezeway.

"How many days are we talking?" I asked.

"Well, today is Sunday, so . . . by Thursday you should be good to go. If you need more time with me, I'll be more than happy to help. I live above you, so I won't be too far if you need me for anything. Get some rest. I'll be back bright and early tomorrow morning."

He waved and made his way up some stairs to the right of my doorway. I closed the door quietly behind me and made sure it was locked and secure. Before going to my room, I looked around the apartment again. It was exactly what I had once imagined my first apartment would look like, which amazed me. I didn't know how tired I was until I laid down on the couch in front of the television to get a feel for it. No sooner than I got comfortable, I fell into a deep sleep.

Chapter 3

Light rapping at the door quickly pulled me out of my sleep, causing me to gasp as if I had been drowning and had just managed to reach the surface to get air. I forgot where I was for a brief moment, so I lay there and stared at the edge of the couch. I tried to suppress the small panic attack I was having. A small clock on the TV stand read eight a.m.

"Julian!"

James called my name through the front door as I squeezed the couch cushion tightly. My heart was racing, and the room felt like it was closing in on me. Out of nowhere, I felt like I was going to be sick.

"Julian, everything will be fine," James assured me. "You're probably feeling a little dizzy right now—maybe even nauseated. I felt the same way a few months ago. It'll pass; I promise. If you can hear me, take a moment to collect yourself, and then let me in. I'll be waiting right outside."

I shut my eyes as I tried to make the room stop shrinking. Taking a few deep breaths, I forced myself to think of something that would calm me down. Images of my parents and old friends appeared, and then I caught a quick glimpse of Alexia's face as well. Before I knew it, I was calm again and didn't feel like I was on a roller coaster or in a crazy fun house. I sat up slowly as I took another deep breath to make sure the episode didn't start again.

"I'll be right there," I called to him.

"Take your time. There's no rush."

I got to my feet just as slowly as when I'd sat up and shuffled to the door. James came in after I'd fumbled with the locks to get the door open, closing it behind himself as I walked over to the small dining room table. I took a seat. He went straight to the fridge and grabbed a bottle of water.

"Here." He slid it across the table and took a seat across from me.

"Thanks." I took a few gulps and immediately felt better. "I forgot where I was, and the knocking pulled me out of my sleep kind of fast," I admitted.

"Ah, it's okay. Like I said, I went through the same thing. For some, it takes a few days to adjust, for others it takes a few hours. Maybe you'll be lucky, and this will be the only episode you have."

I nodded, finished off the rest of the water, and put the cap on the empty bottle. I wasn't as hungry as I had been the night before, so I didn't feel the need to try to fumble through the kitchen to cook anything. "What's the game plan for this week?"

"Today you'll be riding around with me so I can show you the town. Maybe grab a bite to eat a little later if you're hungry. I'll even show you where I work a few days a week. Tomorrow, you'll actually drive your car and follow me around while I drive mine. The day after that, you'll drive me around so I know you've got a general idea of where things are. If you think you'll need more time, I don't mind helping you until you're better adjusted."

"Sounds good. Let me wash up real quick, and I'll be ready."

After throwing away the empty water bottle, I jumped in the shower for a few minutes. The water felt great: lukewarm and calming. From there I quickly brushed my teeth and then went into my room and got dressed. While I was sitting at the edge of my bed, lacing up my shoes, James stood in the doorway and looked on.

"Did you want me to keep calling you Julian, or do you have a nickname? I figured I'd ask you in case you wanted to go by something less formal."

I tied the other shoe and stood up to make sure that they fit snugly, and then I brushed down my jeans and the bottom of my shirt. "You can call me Jules."

"Jules it is."

He stepped to the side as I walked out of the room and shut off the light in the bathroom. Once I was sure everything else was in place, we headed down to his car. I couldn't wait to see what the new town I'd be calling "home" had in store for me.

Chapter 4

That first day with James went pretty well. He showed me the college I'd be attending, a few grocery stores, the park where we'd first met, and other places that would be of use to me. He did everything he could to make sure I wasn't confused or turned around, since he was the one that was driving. I was basically learning and sightseeing. It was obvious that he was concerned that I might be doing more sightseeing than learning. He made it a point to ask me questions to make sure I was paying attention to what he was saying.

"What was the establishment I *just* pointed out to you before we pulled in here?"

We were sitting in an empty parking lot of a shopping center that looked like it had been closed down for years. *For Lease* signs were sitting in all the windows of the buildings on the strip. My face grew hot with embarrassment. I had been too busy people-watching and had agreed to something he'd said at the time. I hoped the place he was asking me about wasn't important.

"Uh . . . an elementary school . . . for . . . the gifted?" I cracked a cheesy smile, but he wasn't amused.

"It was a walk-in clinic—in case something happened and you needed to see a doctor." He sighed. "Listen, Jules. I know this situation and town is new to you and all, but I need you to focus. If you get turned around or into trouble and you don't know where to go for help, and I can't get to you, you're screwed. You know that, right?"

"I do." I unbuckled my seatbelt and slouched in the passenger seat. "I'm a little distracted. I apologize. There's just *so* much to take in, and I want to make sure I don't miss a thing."

James turned the car off and unbuckled his seatbelt as well, turning down the radio as he rolled down both our windows.

"I know it's a lot, but I need you to pay attention to what *I'm* showing you, first. Everything else will fall into place."

"Okay."

"That being said, let's see if you remember all the other places I showed you today. Start from when we first left your apartment this morning."

We sat in the parking lot for an hour so he could quiz me. I only missed a couple of important locations, not including the walk-in clinic. For the most part, I remembered everything I'd seen that morning. I wasn't very good with street names, but I was able to give landmarks to show that I remembered how to get to certain locations. The farthest place he took me was to an indoor flea market, where he worked in one of the booths. He made custom license plates and license plate frames when it was open, which was only three days a week. That's how he made his money. He told me he'd help me find a job as well when I was ready, but until then I'd get whatever help I needed from him and others like us.

After quizzing me, James treated me to lunch at a nearby seafood restaurant. We sat in a booth by a large window that looked out to an inlet. On shore, an old, abandoned ship rested in the mud, covered in barnacles and mold. I had just placed my drink order with the waiter and was reading over the menu. The words "fried eel" caught my attention. James placed his order, as I combed through the menu one last time. He already knew what entrée he wanted, so he didn't hesitate telling the waiter. After giving it some thought, I decided that the fried eel would do, and I placed my order when it was my turn. We waited for our food patiently after the waiter left with the menus.

"So," James began, "you got to see a good portion of the town today. How do you feel about everything?"

"I'm pretty confident that I'll be okay when it comes to getting around." I pulled the wrapper off one of the straws the waiter had left on the table for when our drinks arrived and played with it between my fingertips. "If I forget anything, I can always ask for directions. It'll help me fit in more as the new guy in town and on campus, so it'll be the perfect cover."

"Good thinking. We've still got three days to make sure you'll be all right locally. You should be good to go by the end of the week."

Our drinks arrived first. We both took a few sips while we looked out the window.

"You think there's anything on that ship out there?" I asked.

"Nah, I think it's just a prop. I wouldn't put too much thought into it. Have you thought about what classes you'll want to enroll in?"

Back where I'd originally lived, I had been undecided when it came to my major. I'd planned to start school and get the prerequisites out of the way first. I figured I had two years to decide, so there was no reason to stress over something I was unsure about.

"I think I'll just focus on the prerequisites first," I said. "I'm sure I'll have to take a placement test to keep up with appearances, so that's fine if it comes down to that. I'm more focused on how I'll do when I finally meet her."

"Her?"

"Alexia."

"Is she why you were sent back?"

"Yeah. I'm hoping our first encounter will go smoothly."

"You'll be fine." He assured me as the waiter approached the table to set our meals in front of us. "You wouldn't have been sent back to help her if you couldn't handle it."

We fell silent as we dug into our lunch. I wanted to speed through it because I was so hungry, but the overall smell was enticing, and I wanted to enjoy it as much as I'd enjoyed my food the night before. I took my time and dressed each piece on the plate with lemon juice and horseradish, making sure they were ready for consumption when I was through. The first piece brought tears to my eyes. Not because it tasted delicious, but because I'd overdone it with the horseradish. James laughed as he finished his clam chowder and then started on his main entrée. I laughed as well—once I was able to breathe properly without feeling like I was about to spit fire out my mouth.

After eating, we went back to my apartment. James stayed for a few hours and watched TV with me. The afternoon flew by without our noticing, until we realized it was eight at night. I could see that he was getting tired; his chin kept dropping to his chest while we were watching sports highlights. He was trying to stay awake but was losing the battle.

"It's okay if you want to head back to your place," I offered as I turned off the TV. "We had a long day, so I know you're tired."

He yawned, stretched, and then slowly got to his feet without objecting. I followed him to the door and fumbled with one of the locks again.

"I got it, Jules," he said sleepily as he worked the chain lock I was having trouble with. "You really only need the doorknob lock and the deadbolt. I wouldn't bother with the chain. This is a safe neighborhood, so there's no need to go the extra mile." He patted me on the shoulder as he walked out into the breezeway and took one last stretch as he turned back to me. "You did great today. I knew you'd pick up on things quickly. I'll be back at the same time tomorrow morning."

I gave a quick nod as he made his way up the stairs to his place. Once I'd made sure the door was secure, I went to my room to sleep in the queen-sized bed for the first time. I undressed, slipped into a pair of pajama pants, and then crawled under the downy-soft comforter. After a few minutes of mentally going over everything I'd seen that day, I drifted off to sleep.

The next day, I followed James in my car so I could get the feel of driving around town and go over the places I'd seen the day before. Driving stick shift took a few minutes to get used to again, but after a few stall-outs, it was smooth sailing. That afternoon we caught a movie, grabbed a few sandwiches from the local deli, and then went back to my place for a few hours until he was ready to head home. I was getting the hang of the new routine, which had me feeling more confident about my situation.

Wednesday I drove James around town in my car. He tested me by telling me where he wanted me to take him.

"First, get me to the walk-in clinic. After that, take me to the school, and then pick a spot for us to grab a bite to eat."

I got a little turned around when it came to streets and where to actually turn in to the parking lots, but in the end I did an amazing job. We ended up at a pizzeria that I had been thinking about since I'd seen it Monday afternoon. We both got a slice of pizza and a drink and then headed back to my place to play some video games. I whipped up some dinner later that evening as a friendly gesture, since James had been paying for our food for the past four days. After he finished eating, he thanked me and got ready to leave for the night. He let me know that he wouldn't be by on Thursday morning because he had something important to do, but he'd stop by later that afternoon.

"You should drop by the registration building on campus tomorrow and get your class schedule taken care of," he suggested.

I thought about it and figured that was a good idea. "I think I'll do that. Who do I speak to when I get there?"

James dug in his pants pocket and pulled out a business card. He handed it to me, and I inspected it. The school's name and logo was printed across the front, with a building and office number scribbled on the back.

"She knows you're here, so you'll be in and out with no issues."

"You've been so thorough with all this."

"Well you're the first person I've helped with this sort of thing, so I want to make sure I'm doing the best job I can," he pointed out.

Thursday morning I woke up a little after seven. After taking a quick shower and throwing on some clothes, I rummaged through the fridge, trying to decide on what I wanted to eat. I figured a quick fried egg and some juice would tide me over for a few hours. I grabbed an egg from the carton and a container of orange juice and closed the door behind me with my foot. It only took me a minute or two to find the frying pan I needed and grab a drinking glass. The egg came out perfect, just the way my mother taught me to make it. The juice tasted extra fresh and helped me to wake up a little more. By the time I'd finished cleaning up after myself and had brushed my teeth, it was

8:30. I grabbed the card James had given me the night before and headed out to enroll in classes.

It only took me a few minutes to reach the campus. There were a few cars scattered here and there, but it wasn't packed like it had been when we'd driven by on Monday and Wednesday. I explored the campus for a few minutes to get a feel for everything before heading to the counselor's office. Not many people were walking around, so I assumed classes were in session. I secretly hoped I'd run into Alexia, but the couple of students I did see didn't look like the person G had showed me in the pond on Sunday. When I figured I had made it around the entire campus, I walked into the registration building and found the office that was written on the back of the card.

I knocked quietly before walking in to speak to the elderly woman sitting behind a large wooden desk. She looked up from what she was doing, gazed at me through her thick bifocals, and gestured for me to take a seat in front of her. I did as I was instructed, sinking into one of the plush blue chairs. I tried finding a plaque with her name on it, but I couldn't find one. She wasn't wearing a name tag either, so for me she was just "the counselor lady." The smell of mothballs and green tea hung in the air.

"Julian Reed?"

"Yes," I confirmed.

She began going through a small stack of folders sitting to the right of her desk. It was obvious that she was someone who preferred to get down to business. I wasn't sure if she was only this way with people like me or with everyone she handled. I figured it was for the best, since I was still a little tired and wanted to get more sleep anyway. Once she'd found what I assumed was my file, she grabbed a pen from one of the desk drawers.

"Freshman?"

"Yes."

She scribbled with the pen. "Full-time or part-time?"

"Full-time should be fine."

More scribbling. "Decided or undecided in regards to your major?"

"Undecided for now."

Again with the scribbling.

After making a few extra marks and keying some information into her computer, she printed out my class schedule and handed it to me along with a student ID. I looked it over to see what day I started and what classes I had. Just as I'd thought would happen, I was enrolled in prerequisite courses. The picture on my student ID matched the one that was on my driver's license.

"Come to me with any questions or concerns while you attend here," the counselor instructed, "especially if you need time away for anything."

"Thank you. I'm sorry, I don't know your name."

"My name isn't important. Just remember this office when or if you need anything school-related." She went back to what she'd been doing when I first arrived and didn't say another word.

"Thanks again," I said.

She nodded, not looking away from her papers.

When I got home, it was still pretty early, so I hung my class schedule on the refrigerator door, after kicking off my sneakers behind the couch. I wasn't sure what time James would be coming by, so I figured it'd be best to catch a quick nap in the front room, in case he arrived while I was sleeping. I wanted to hear it when he knocked. I jumped over the back of the couch and landed right in the center of it, which caused a few of the throw pillows to fall on the floor. I grabbed the one that I'd fallen asleep with on my first night in the apartment, and I curled up with it. Within minutes, I was out like a light.

Chapter 5

James arrived in what felt like five minutes after I shut my eyes, when in reality it was hours later, with a bag of tacos in tow. He herded me down to his car after I freshened up from my nap and put my sneakers on. He didn't tell me where we were going, except that it was a place where he liked to go to sit and have some alone time.

"Is this somewhere I need to remember for any particular reason?" I asked as I put my seat belt on.

He handed me the bag of tacos as he got into the driver's seat and started the car. The smell crept up my nostrils and caused my stomach to growl. I'd only had the small breakfast I'd made to tide me over the entire day, so I was grateful that he'd thought to bring food with him.

"Nope. I mean, if you *want* to remember, then that's fine. I'm sure you'll find your own place to have some down time. This isn't something that'll hurt you if you don't remember where it is."

The sun was slowly setting as he pulled into the parking lot of a small beach, parked near a small restroom stall, and shut the car off. There weren't many cars there, so at first I wasn't sure if it was okay to be there that late.

He must have sensed what I was feeling, as he grabbed the bag of tacos from my lap and said, "Don't worry. We won't get into trouble or anything."

I followed behind him slowly as we walked up a few steps to a wooden deck that overlooked the beach. We stopped briefly at the top, and I was surprised to see that there were groups of people setting up small bonfires for when the sun set completely. I realized at that moment that there wasn't much I had to worry about when I was with James. It was obvious that he wouldn't steer me the wrong way.

"Neat, huh?" he chuckled. We walked down the steps that led to the sand and the ocean.

"Are they like *us*?"

"Well, technically, *I'm* not like *you*, so it's hard to have a straight answer for that."

We found a spot between two groups that were starting to light the wood they'd gathered. None of them paid us any attention as we got settled in the sand. I looked on as James dug into the bag and handed me two tacos. They were still warm; I couldn't wait to bite into one.

We enjoyed our food as we watched stars appear slowly in the ink-blue sky above the ocean. The groups around us were quietly talking amongst themselves as they roasted marshmallows. No one approached us or asked questions.

"Do you always come here alone?" I balled up the empty taco wrappers and threw them into the bag we'd brought them in.

"I do." James tossed aside a bright-colored shell that was next to him, and started digging into a small sand mound that was under it. After a couple of seconds, he pulled a folded piece of paper from the hole he'd dug. I watched as he unfolded it and read what looked like a letter. When he was finished, he folded it back up and shoved it into his back pocket.

"And that was?" I inquired.

"A list." He said nonchalantly.

"What's a list doing all the way out here, buried in the sand? It must not be all that important if it was left at the beach." I joked.

He looked out to the ocean and didn't respond. I wasn't sure if he was purposely not answering me so I'd stop asking questions, or if he was thinking of something to come back with. I immediately felt bad when I realized I might have offended him. If that was the case, I wanted to correct it.

"Listen, if you don't want to talk about it, I get it."

He still didn't say anything.

I looked out to the ocean as well after a moment and listened to the waves. The sky was filled with stars now with the random cloud that slowly coasted by. I tried to find a star that would be brighter than the others to see if it would twinkle at me like the one on Sunday night, but I didn't see anything. I found the Big Dipper and a few other constellations, though, so I was okay with that.

"Jules . . . remember when I said I'm technically not like you?"

I was relieved when he finally broke the silence. "Yeah, but I didn't think anything of it. What'd you mean by that?"

James crossed his legs out in front of him to get more comfortable, tossed his taco wrapper into the bag, and pushed sand back into the hole he'd dug. He dusted off his hands and gave me a side glance, coupled with a crooked smile.

"I *almost* died once," he started. "I didn't fully transition and cross over like you. I just had a near-death experience. I was out long enough to meet the one in charge of things." He pointed up at a small cluster of stars. "G spoke to me while I was there and gave me something to do when I came to."

I was speechless.

"That list I pulled out of the sand has to do with something . . . some*one*. I've been looking out for her for a little over two months now. She comes here a few times a week and buries letters or lists in the sand in random locations. I collect them to make sure everything is okay, until it's time for me to make my presence known. I'm sure it won't be long now before I swoop in and save the day," James smiled to himself.

"How'd it happen?" I turned my entire body, so I was looking at him as he spoke.

"What? My brush with death?"

I nodded.

"I drowned in this very ocean when summer vacation started after my high school graduation. I was out too far and was too stupid to listen to the rip current warnings. I got pulled under and couldn't get back to the surface for air. I thought I was finished. When I opened my eyes I was at a beach like this one and was greeted by G.

"We walked for what felt like days, just talking and joking, going through some memories of mine and whatnot. G told me about this girl that was having some personal problems, which, of course, made me feel bad, you know? So I asked what I could do to help. After G explained her dilemma, and made sure I understood what I'd have to do, I woke up in the hospital. Apparently, I had been in a coma for a couple of weeks. Ever since then, I've been able to tell if someone is . . . well, *different*."

"Different in what sense?" I asked curiously.

"I can usually tell if someone passed away and came back, like you, or just had a near-death experience, like me."

"Does your family know about your special sense?"

"Yeah, right." He scooped up the bag of empty taco wrappers and got to his feet. "My parents would send me to a mental institute or something. Besides, G told me they don't need to know. Not everyone picks up a special gift after that sort of incident, so it's pretty cool when you think about it."

"Right." I got to my feet as well. "I appreciate you sharing that story with me."

"Don't mention it." He shrugged as he led me back to the car. "It's nice to have someone to talk to about it. It helps."

Once we got back to our apartment complex, we went up to his place to relax and talk some more before I turned in for the night. He showed me most of, if not all, the letters and lists he had been collecting from the girl he'd been looking after. He had so many, it seemed as though he'd been collecting them for a few years. There was a mixture of letters and lists that said what she was looking for in a guy she'd want to date. I'd had friends who did that sort of thing back home, but I didn't think much of it then. I figured it was their personal way of getting out their frustrations when they were in a relationship with someone who wasn't up to par.

"What's her name?" I folded up the last letter he let me read and dropped it back into the wooden box he kept them in.

"Alora," he sighed.

"Going by what I've read, she seems nice."

"She *is* nice. But she's with this guy that just—" James started choking an invisible throat in the air with his hands to show his dislike for the guy in question. "You know how it goes with some relationships, right? Everything is amazing in the beginning, and then someone gets lazy. It's a real shame that someone like her got mixed up with someone like him. She deserves better."

"And you're the better?" I guessed.

"That I am, sir."

He took the box away from me and placed it under the coffee table that was between us and the TV.

"I may not be *everything* she's looking for, but I know I can take better care of her than that guy she's with. I've been keeping my distance and collecting what she buries at the beach to keep tabs on what's going on. I think the relationship is almost at its breaking point, so I'm just being patient."

You could hear in his voice that he was passionate about making the wrong in Alora's life very right. I admired his drive.

"Why don't you introduce yourself to her now?" I asked.

"Because knowing me, I'd convince her to dump the zero and get with a hero. I wouldn't put it to her like *that* since that's a pretty corny line, but you get what I'm saying. I can't be any kind of influence on her decisions when it comes to the relationship she's in. If they break up, it has to be because one of them decided they've had enough. To be honest, I'm concerned that someone else will step in before I can. G assured me that won't happen, though, so I'm trying not to stress over it. Anyway . . . how'd your trip to the registration building go?" James asked. "Did you get your classes?"

I had managed to grab my class schedule on the way out the door when he came to get me that evening so I could show it to him. He read it over and smiled.

"So you're in . . . Intermediate Algebra, Marine Biology, Basic Economics, and World Literature, huh? You've got a full course load. Did you pick any of these?"

"No, the counselor picked them for me."

"You should go to the campus tomorrow and find these classes so you know where you're going next week. You may get lucky and bump into Alexia while you're there, so you should rest up."

When he suggested that I get a good night's sleep, we both got off the couch and made our way to the door so I could head down to my apartment.

"I was kind of hoping to see her today," I said, "but luck wasn't on my side. Also, the counselor you referred me to was a bit . . . cold."

"Ah, don't mind her." He handed my schedule back to me. "She's old and ready for her time to be called home. I heard that for some people, the older they get, the more they 'see.' So she's kind of like me, minus the near-death fiasco. She'll do anything and everything for you, though, until she passes on. Hopefully, when that time comes, someone will take her place that'll be just as good as she is."

"Hopefully."

I started to feel a little anxious at the thought of meeting Alexia for the first time. It must have shown on my face.

"I took time off from school this week to help you," James informed me. "The only thing you'll have to do is talk to her if you run into each other. There's a *chance* that might happen, so I wouldn't get your hopes up if I were you. Get there good and early, and take your time to find your classes. If you see her, then that's great. If you don't, then you definitely will on Monday."

"Where will you be if I need you for anything?"

"I'll either be here or at the beach until I have to head to work. Alora usually goes there the same time every couple of days, so I try to arrive a little after she leaves so I can dig up what she buried. By the way, I picked this up for you."

He dug into his back pocket and handed me a small cell phone. It was basic, but it'd get the job done if I needed to call him.

"My number is already saved in the contact list." He went to the kitchen, grabbed the charger that was resting on the counter, placed it in my hand, and slipped me forty dollars in case of emergencies.

"You're *sure* you'll be around if I need you?"

"If something happens—good, bad, or indifferent—and you need help or anything, call me. No matter where I am, I'll find a way to get to you. Now go get some sleep."

He opened the door for me, and I walked out. I stood in the breezeway as I inspected the phone.

"Hey, Jules,"

I looked up from what I was doing.

"Don't put so much thought into tomorrow; just let things flow."

Easier said than done.

Chapter 6

I plugged the phone into the charger next to the bed as I got ready to go to sleep. James was right; things would go well tomorrow, as long as I didn't put so much thought into it. He seemed to be an optimistic person and, most likely, wanted me to be the same way. I was more of a realist, so being excited about something when there could be different outcomes didn't come easy for me.

Crawling under the comforter, I tried to slow my racing thoughts.

Maybe, if I spoke to G, I'd feel better.

I shut my eyes and began talking aloud quietly, hoping I'd be heard. I talked about how things were going with James and how helpful he had been all week; about the food I'd eaten and how I'd made breakfast; about the beach . . . and about how nervous I was about meeting Alexia.

I heard what sounded like a small child giggling and opened my eyes mid-sentence. I was surprised to find that I wasn't in my apartment anymore, but at the park I'd arrived at Sunday. The small girl who had helped me twice before was running around, blowing bubbles in the moonlight. Her hair was flowing behind her as she giggled and popped them, only to blow more. I was smiling at how carefree she was, when suddenly she stopped and looked at me.

"Jax!" She closed the red bottle of bubbles, shoved it into one of her dress pockets, and ran up to me. She wrapped herself around my waist and gave me a huge hug. "I have something for you," she whispered.

She dug into a small pocket in her white dress and handed me what looked to be a folded-up picture. I opened it and saw that it was of Alexia. She was sitting alone in a sundress under a willow tree in the very park we were in. Upon turning the picture over, I found that her first and last names were written on the back in script: *Alexia Waters.*

I walked over to a nearby bench, still staring at the picture as the little girl followed close behind. I took a seat, and she sat next to me.

"G told me to give that to you so you'd remember what she looked like," she stared at the picture as well.

"Can I take it with me? I mean, am I *really* here at the park right now, or am I dreaming?"

"You're dreaming," she informed me. "As long as you're asleep, you'll have the picture, but you won't have it with you when you wake up. The ability to travel to different locations and between worlds while you dream was the gift that was given to you when you came back. You can also get in contact with us this way. Just talk or think about something specific as you drift off to sleep. Either G will show up or I will, okay?"

I gave her a one-armed hug, and she wrapped herself around my waist again to hug me back. "Thanks. And tell G that I said thanks too."

"Okay. I'm going back to playing with my bubbles now. See you later, Jax!" She hopped off the bench and ran to a nearby play area.

I continued to study the picture to make sure I would recognize Alexia if I saw her on campus the next day.

When I was sure I'd remember her face, I closed my eyes and folded the picture up. A loud buzzing noise flooded my ears and caused my eyes to fly open. I was in my room again, staring at the ceiling. A little sunlight was pouring through the bedroom window onto the comforter I was under, and the alarm read 8:30 a.m. I didn't hesitate to get up and start getting ready to head to school.

When I arrived, I parked under a large willow tree on the far side of the campus. I was happy that I stumbled across that type of tree in particular. It reminded me of my favorite spot where I used to sit before I was given the chance to come back to the world of the living. *I should find the one I saw in the picture last night,* I thought. I started walking around to find the classes I'd be attending on Mondays, Wednesdays, and Fridays, following the campus map that was printed on the back of my schedule. Algebra was the first one I located. When I approached the door to take a peek into the classroom, I found a note taped to it to let students know that class was cancelled because the instructor was out sick. *That sucks for people who drove out here, not knowing they wouldn't have class. Especially if this was their only class for the day.*

Soon after that, I found my biology class. It was in the building right across from the one I was in. Those two classes alone only took a total of five minutes to locate, so I felt like I was rushing. It took me a little longer to find the two classes I'd be taking on Tuesdays and Thursdays.

That was when I realized that the campus was bigger than I'd originally thought it was. I was determined to find them without any help, which took my mind off of Alexia.

After locating my economics class, I found my literature class. That was it. I'd found all of them in under an hour. I was a little proud of myself and a little disappointed. I had been hoping for more of a challenge. I put the schedule into my back pocket and walked toward the glass double doors so I could head home, but I froze just as I was about to go outside.

It was her.

Alexia coasted by the building without noticing me standing inside the dimly lit hallway. After waiting a few seconds to let her get further away, I crept up to the doors to watch where she was going. She was walking down the same beaten-down grass trail I had used to get to the other buildings. She made her way to the courtyard, chose a table, and got her things situated. Then she sat down and started leafing through a notebook.

I stepped away from the doors, trying to decide what I should do. *Do I wait for her to go to her car? Should I go sit with her? I can't stand here and stare at her; that'd be creepy . . .*

"Pull yourself together," I said aloud, giving myself a pep talk. "You can do this. It isn't rocket science. You're just striking up a conversation with someone you're here to help." I peeked through the door again and saw that she was talking on the phone. The conversation didn't last long. Then her attention went from what looked like coloring on her notebook to two couples walking into the courtyard across the way.

That was when I decided to make my way over to her.

I gave my hair a quick brush with my hand and exited the building. My pace wasn't too fast or too slow. The closer I got to her table, the more I could feel my heart beating in my throat. When I finally reached her, she was still looking at the other students across the courtyard. I squared my shoulders and took a deep breath, clearing my throat to get her attention. When she gazed up at me, I spoke.

"Mind if I sit here?"

She looked me over quickly, only to shrug one of her shoulders at my inquiry. "Not at all," she answered coolly as she went back to lightly shading what looked to be a drawing of a marble.

"Thanks," I said. I got settled next to her, as she continued her shading. We both sat quietly, as I tried to come up with something else to say.

Chapter 7

"I'm heading out!" I called, pausing before walking out the front door. I waited for a response from one of my parents. I wanted to make sure someone heard me say I was leaving for the day.

"Good luck on your quiz, Marbles!" my father called from the kitchen.

Marbles, I thought. *I wish they'd call me Alexia. And I'll need more than luck to pass this quiz.*

I already hated college, and it was only the second week. During the first week, I recognized a few people wandering around on campus from the junior high and high school I'd graduated from. They recognized me too but looked through me like I didn't exist. When I walked into each class, I smiled at anyone I made eye contact with; hoping things would be less weird as the week went by. After the first few days, though, it was obvious that a lot of people I had once considered friends or at least close associates had changed over the summer. By the end of the week, I hated having to go to school.

I had thought that my best friend since kindergarten, Alora, would have come around over the summer, and we'd be partners in crime on campus in the fall. I'd stopped dating someone in our junior year of high school—around the same time she'd started dating a guy named Jordan. As time passed, she became more distant because of him. We checked in on each other here and there for a while, but we didn't hang out the way we'd used to. I didn't like him; but if he made her happy, then there wasn't much I could say. I saw her going from class to class the week before, but she never saw me, or if she did, I couldn't tell. I didn't bother attempting to chase her down. Instead, I tried to get by without her.

I began looking forward to Fridays the first week that college started. I was excited about the school week coming to a close, because I was tired of stressing out about socializing while I was there. When I woke up on this particular Friday morning, though, things felt "off"—in a good way. I couldn't put my finger on it, but I felt the difference the moment I rolled out of bed and started getting dressed. I tried not to put too much thought into it, in case nothing happened out of the norm.

I parked in my usual spot under a large willow tree on the far side of the campus next to another car. I had my first algebra quiz of the semester that morning, and I hadn't studied any of the material for it. The professor hadn't hesitated to dive right into the syllabus after passing it out to everyone the first day of class. I made it a point to arrive earlier than usual to study a little. After grabbing my books and purse, I locked my car and made my way between two buildings down the beaten-down grass trail made by students who had passed through before me.

I inhaled deeply through my nose to take in the smell of freshly cut hedges. The sky seemed a little bit bluer, and there wasn't a cloud in sight. There was still some morning dew on the blades of grass, which made the whole landscape look like a sea of emeralds in the sun. I approached a small grated table in the courtyard and set my books down, along with my purse. I took a seat on the long, concrete block that served as the bench and began to flip through some math notes.

After a minute or two of blankly staring at foreign symbols and equations in front of me, I figured that I would just wing the quiz. I shut my notebook and began to scribble my name in cursive, over and over on the cover. I loved my name: Alexia. Some of my family members, professors, and coworkers called me Alex for short. I paused for a second and looked at my reflection in one of the large windows on the building across from me. I smiled at myself and went back to what I was doing.

The table suddenly began to vibrate lightly under my purse. I reached into it and pulled out my cell phone. Taking a quick glance at the caller ID before answering it, I saw that it was my parents calling. I pressed the answer button, and placed it gently to my right ear.

"Hello?" I answered, as if I didn't know it was one of them calling.

"Marbles, you didn't call and tell us you made it to school. Are you there yet?" my mother questioned.

"Can't you just call me Alex instead of Marbles?" I asked, not answering her initial question. "Or by my full first name even? You know: the one I was given at birth?"

"Why?" she said. "You've been obsessed with marbles since you were a little girl, so it suits you. I don't see what the big deal is. I can always call you by some other cute nickname, you know."

"Ugh, no. Marbles is fine. And yes, I'm at school."

"Good. I just wanted to make sure you got there safely. I'll talk to you later," she cooed.

I hung up the phone, set it next to my purse, and continued with my scribbling. I went from writing my name to drawing little blue marbles all over the cover. They truly were my obsession—the colors, the cool feel of them in the palms of my hands, the sound they made when they hit each other when playing a game of marbles. It was an odd obsession, granted, but it was *my* obsession. That was all that mattered to me.

Laughter from other students entering from the other side of the courtyard caused me to stop what I was doing and direct my attention to them. Two couples were approaching an empty table. The pairs were holding hands as they all laughed together at whatever they were talking about, taking seats at the round concrete table they chose. I slouched a little and gazed at them as they got situated with their books, bags, and Styrofoam coffee cups.

I recognized one of the couples: Matt and Samantha. Everyone called her Sam. When we were in elementary school and junior high, we all used to hang out with each other—back when they were just friends and nothing more. When we got to high school, they caught feelings for each other and started dating. Then Alora ended up in a relationship, and I pretty much fell out of the loop. Since I wasn't dating anyone, I didn't like the idea of being the third wheel, so I kept my distance. I figured I'd try to catch up with them at some point, since I hadn't seen them all summer or when the fall semester started. I knew that *they*, at least, would take the time to find out how I was doing. Alora, on the other hand, would probably find some excuse to be somewhere else. The thought of it upset me so much it caused my stomach to feel like it was producing molten lava.

My people-watching session was interrupted when I heard someone clear his throat to get my attention. I ended up making eye contact with someone I hadn't seen around campus before.

"Mind if I sit here?" the stranger asked.

I quickly looked him over, only to shrug at his inquiry. "Not at all," I answered coolly as I went back to lightly shading in the marble picture I'd drawn a moment earlier.

"Thanks," he said.

I watched him with my peripheral vision as he took a seat next to me. Once he was settled, we both sat silently as I continued to shade in my drawing. I ended up watching the couples at the other table again when Sam let out one of her signature high-pitched giggles. They were all sitting on the table now as they sipped on their drinks.

"Nice, huh? You know, being a part of a tight-knit group and all?" the stranger asked, breaking the silence with his smooth voice.

"It's okay," I replied, trying to sound indifferent to what was happening across the courtyard. I shifted my notebook a little and kept my attention on the couples across the way, kind of hoping that he would go away—but also kind of hoping he would stay.

"I think it's great. I mean, I'm sure it isn't easy maintaining relationships when you first start school and all, you know? People get involved with each other over the summer, friends move away . . ."

"Or they just forget about you," I grumbled.

"That too." He smiled nervously.

I thought about how I must have come across to him for a moment and stopped watching what was going on at the other table. "I'm sorry," I said. "I didn't mean to snap at you or anything. I was thinking about this same topic before you sat down, and I was starting to feel a little bitter about it."

"It's okay," he said. "I'm sure you didn't mean anything by it. I'm sorry I kind of pushed the subject."

I gave a courteous nod to show I accepted his apology and then awkwardly started leafing through my math notes.

"So, what's your name?" he asked.

My thoughts suddenly began to race. The inquiry was unexpected; my stomach was tying up in knots from nervousness. I wanted to answer him, but for whatever reason, it felt like I'd forgotten my name altogether. I smiled sheepishly, trying to remain calm as I struggled so very hard to remember the answer to such a simple question. This was exactly why I hated my social anxiety. It caused me to forget how to do the simple things: like how to speak or even breathe. Thinking of something else as quickly as I could usually helped me. I inhaled deeply through my nose, hoping he didn't notice, and focused on something other than his question.

He seems nice—the key word being seems—*based on his outer appearance, of course. He's well put-together and decent-looking; I can't deny that. And he smells nice. I wonder what cologne he's wearing. Should I ask him? Wait, I can't; that'd be answering a question with a question. Oh God, I still haven't answered his question!*

After a few seconds of staring at him, it was more like I was staring *through* him, as if he weren't there. It became painfully obvious that I was over-thinking the situation when he smiled and chuckled lightly.

"I hope that wasn't too forward of me. It would help our small talk if we knew each other's name."

Snap out of it!

"Alexia. But you can call me Alex," I managed to finally get out.

A light breeze rustled some of the loose papers I had inside my notebook. I placed my hand on it lightly to make sure they didn't blow away.

"Do you sit here and people-watch often, Alex?" he asked.

"No, I got here a little early to do some light studying and wanted to sit somewhere nice. Ever since school started, I've been sitting in my car when I arrive to look over my class notes, so I figured this would be a nice change of scenery."

I realized that I didn't feel nervous like I had when he'd first started talking to me. I also found that I was able to keep eye contact with him; something I usually had a hard time doing when it came to talking to strangers. I felt more at ease when I took note of how friendly his eyes were.

There was no reason for me to feel the way I did in the beginning. He just caught me off guard.

"Well, I'm glad I ran into you," he said. "I came here this morning to find my classes. I start on Monday. I moved here earlier this week, so I'm still learning my way around and everything."

"Oh, nice. Where'd you move from?"

"California," he said with a bit of hesitation.

"I heard it's beautiful over there. Did you move here with your parents, on your own, or with friends?"

"Um, I'm here alone. I mean, I have a friend that lives above me in my apartment complex, but he didn't move here with me." Before I could ask him any more questions, he quickly changed the subject. "My name is Julian, by the way. Jules, for short."

He extended his right hand to me, so I placed mine into it gingerly. I smiled lightly as he gave it a gentle squeeze. I didn't think too much into the abrupt topic change, figuring that if it was something he wanted to talk about, he would have. It was probably something personal he didn't want to discuss with a stranger anyway, so I respected that.

"Nice to meet you Julian," I said.

"Jules," he insisted.

Maybe this is why I felt "off" when I woke up, I thought, *because I was going to have this encounter.* Seconds later I realized that I was still holding his hand. I had zoned out briefly as I thought about how flighty I'd felt as I was getting ready for school that morning. I gave his hand an extra squeeze.

"Right. Nice to meet you, Jules." I smiled.

Chapter 8

He slid a little closer to me, slowly letting go of my hand. His decision to move closer would have caused me to scoot away any other day. But I stayed put and went along with it, since I didn't feel the slightest bit uncomfortable with him entering my personal space.

"Do your friends call you Alexia or Alex?" he asked.

"It all depends on the person, really, but personally I prefer being called Alex. I don't have many friends, so it kind of doesn't matter. I had three close friends, but two are dating each other, so I rarely see either of them.

They're pretty much attached at the hip. The other is having relationship problems, so she's been MIA," I mumbled.

"I'm sorry to hear that."

"It's okay. It's my own fault that I'm not a real people person outside of those three. I tend to keep to myself most of the time anyway. Plus, with the way the first week of school went, I just don't see the point in being a social butterfly when I'm here."

"Well, you're doing fine with me, and we've just met. I'd say that you've acquired a new friend . . . or at least an acquaintance. Wouldn't you?"

I thought about it for a moment. "I guess you could say that." We smiled at each other warmly, just taking in the moment of two complete strangers having a nice conversation.

"You want to hear something funny?" he offered.

"Sure."

"It's a strange icebreaker, but—okay, my real name is Julian, right? A few people call me Jules. But my parents and family members insist on calling me the strangest nickname—one I acquired when I was a kid."

"Really?" I turned my entire body to face him, placing my left leg under me to get a little more comfortable.

"Yeah. They insist on calling me Jax."

Our attention briefly went back to the couples across the courtyard when we both heard one last high-pitched giggle from Sam. They all rose to their feet and began to walk to a far-off building.

"That's a unique nickname," I said. "Why do they call you that?"

"My dad says it's because it's been my favorite game ever since I learned how to play. For a while, we would play a few rounds while my mom was at work. The way it's spelled isn't the traditional way of spelling the actual game, but my dad said that makes it different. It's silly, I know," he said with a light shrug.

I felt myself smiling on the inside. How crazy was it that we had something so unique in common? "That's . . . neat." I caught myself before saying that it sounded like the same origin as my own family nickname. Instead, I ran my hand through my hair to make sure it was lying down neatly. I didn't want to say anything about the coincidence. No sooner did I make that decision than he asked about it.

"What about you? I'm sure you have a family nickname."

"Well, my parents call me Marbles," I began, but I was cut off by his light chuckling. I usually got offended when people laughed at my nickname, but it didn't even pinch a nerve this time. "What's so funny?"

"I wasn't laughing *at* you or anything. I heard the name and thought to myself, *That really suits her.*"

"Marbles was my favorite game as a kid, and I kind of have this weird obsession with them. They just come in so many different sizes and colors. I can't help but be obsessed with them." I smiled.

"I hear you," he started, but before he could continue, my phone vibrated, signaling that I'd received a text.

I grabbed it and took a look at the message that was across the screen. An unknown number had sent me my horoscope for the day. "I don't remember signing up for notifications like this," I said to myself. I clicked on the link in the text to open the message. Jules waited patiently as I watched the message load on my phone. It finally appeared on a bright-green background, showing my zodiac sign and the date. The horoscope was short and simple. It also gave me goose bumps.

You'll meet a beautiful, smart, and loving person today. Don't let them pass you by!

I swallowed so hard, it felt like everyone on campus should have heard it.

"Everything okay?" Jules asked. "You look like you just saw a ghost."

I lowered my phone and tried to erase the look of shock from my face. *This can't be possible. It's too coincidental.*

"Alex?"

I snapped out of it and flashed a quick smile. "Everything's fine. It was just . . . a message from my service provider. They were . . . verifying that they received my payment for my bill this month." I closed the message, noticing how much time had passed. It was already a quarter after ten; I was fifteen minutes late to class. "Great, I'm late for this quiz," I moaned as my stomach sank. "I'll be lucky if the professor still lets me take it."

"For which class?" Jules pulled a piece of paper out his back pocket and unfolded it, sliding it over to me so I could take a look at it. It was his schedule. I quickly skimmed it, and learned that he was in the same Intermediate Algebra class as me. I pointed to it, sliding it back over to him.

"I saw a sign on the door this morning that said the class was cancelled today."

I sighed in relief when he told me that, only to realize that I'd driven to the campus for a class I didn't even have to attend. And I only had the one class that day. "Ugh . . . I drove all the way here for nothing. It would have been nice to have been able to sleep in this morning or not skip breakfast, since I wanted to get here early to study." My stomach grumbled as I griped.

"I know you just met me and everything, but I wouldn't mind treating you to breakfast, if that's okay."

"I don't know . . ."

"I'll completely understand if you don't feel comfortable with that."

I looked him in the eye, trying to see if he was the kind of person I should worry about. I liked to think that I was good at reading people. For the most part, I was always spot-on when it came to knowing whether a person was someone I wanted to get to know, or someone I needed to avoid. I wasn't getting any bad vibes from him, but I wanted to play it safe.

"We can grab some breakfast to go and eat at the park," I suggested. "The weather's nice. We can go to my favorite spot so we can talk some more."

"I'd like that."

"Perfect!" I went to pick up my books, but before I could, Jules scooped them up to carry them for me. All I had to worry about was my purse.

"Allow me," he offered.

As he held my books under one of his arms, we both got up from the table to make our way to our cars.

"Where did you park?" he asked.

"Over in the parking lot under the large willow tree." I pointed in the general direction we'd have to go to get there.

"Nice. I parked there too."

We walked side-by-side down the path I'd taken earlier that morning to sit in the courtyard. It felt weird not carrying my own books. No one had ever offered to do that for me.

"Are you sure you're okay with carrying my stuff?" I asked. "I can do it myself." I looked up at him as we walked.

"I insist." He said with a warm smile.

Apparently, the car I'd backed in next to that morning was his. I readied my car fob as he followed me around to the back of it and waited for me to pop the trunk. I opened it, watching as he placed my stuff on top of my work apron and uniform inside a Rubbermaid container. I used it to keep my books from sliding around in the trunk while I was driving.

"So," Jules said, "do you want to follow me in your car, or would you like to ride with me?"

I gave it a quick thought. "Well, we can take my car—if you're comfortable with that, of course."

"Sure, that's fine. Just let me grab some cash real quick, and then we can go."

He closed the trunk for me and went over to his car as I got into the driver's seat of mine. He didn't take long to grab what he needed and slide into the passenger seat, shutting the door softly. After putting our seatbelts on, I put the car in gear, and drove to the diner closest to the park to grab some food to go. Afterward, we drove to the park. We didn't speak the entire way there, but I didn't mind. Having company, for once, was enough for me.

Chapter 9

Jules followed close behind me as we trekked across a large grass field toward the park's lake. I led him up a decent-sized hill with a large willow tree at the top that looked over it. People were jogging on the concrete path that went around the entire lake, while others relaxed on grassy knolls near small oak trees, bushes, and play areas.

Once we got to the top, he placed the plastic bag full of food at the base of the tree. I opened the blanket I'd taken from the backseat of my car and spread it out so we could sit on it. After getting everything ready, we both sat and ate while we watched people use small paddle boats to navigate around in the water. Some kids were screeching at the top of their lungs as they tried to get small kites into the air.

"Do you sit *here* and people-watch often?" Jules asked. He bit into a piece of toast and then took a sip of orange juice.

"I do," I answered, covering my full mouth with my hand. "It's really nice here this time of year. The tree provides cool shade, and the breeze feels amazing up here when there is one. I also love willow trees." I dropped my plastic fork in the empty container that had once housed four slices of French toast and some sausage links.

"Me too."

"How long have you been here again?" I asked.

"I got here Sunday, so almost a week." He reached over and grabbed my empty food container, dropping it into the bag we'd brought it in.

"Well, how do you like it here so far?"

He paused briefly from cleaning up around us and thought about it. It seemed as though I'd stirred up a memory that he was watching like a small movie right in front of him. He looked a little sad, but I could see that he was smiling with his eyes at the same time.

"So far, it's pretty nice. My friend that lives above me is cool. And then I met you today, so that helps a little more with the transition and all."

"That's good. I'm glad you're settling in. Do you keep in touch with your family a lot since you've moved here?"

"Not really. When I left, it was pretty sudden and unexpected, so they're still upset about it. I don't bother them too much, which is probably for the best."

"I see."

He finished throwing all the empty containers into the bag. He then put a corner of the blanket over it so it wouldn't blow away. I didn't feel comfortable asking him about where he was from or about his family anymore, since he didn't seem comfortable talking about it. I quickly thought of something else to talk about, since I wanted to learn more about him.

"Why do *you* like willows?" I asked.

"They're the best trees for climbing and taking naps under, of course." He said matter-of-factly.

"I've never climbed a tree before. I'd hate to get up there and get stuck. Plus, I have a small fear of heights."

"You're missing out on an amazing view of the entire park because of that 'small fear,'" he said.

I looked up through the branches at the rays of light that were pouring through them, figuring he was probably right about the view.

"We can climb it together, if you'd like, since I'm here," he offered.

"I don't know . . ."

"I swear we won't go too high. I see the perfect branch we can sit on." He pointed to one that looked to have an easy way up to it and an easy way back down. I still wasn't sure, though.

Without warning, he got up and started to scale the side of the tree to the nearest branch. He sat on it once he got there, letting his legs swing. His shoe was untied, so I slapped at the white shoelace when I got to my feet.

"We'll take it slow," he said. "Come on. Try to get up to this branch to start." He tied his shoe as he waited for me to come up.

I watched as loose bark drifted down to the blanket as he scooted over a little to give me room to sit next to him. I counted to three in my head and jumped as high as I could to grab one of the blunt tree knobs that were just within reach. It was big enough for me to get both hands around it. I reached over, grabbed the branch he was sitting on, and hung there briefly.

"Hang on, I've got you." Jules grabbed one of my arms and pulled me up as I pulled myself up with the other. A few seconds later, I was sitting next to him on the branch, catching my breath.

"Not so bad, right?"

"I guess not."

"All right. To the next branch!"

He got up excitedly, stepped over me, and climbed to the second branch above our heads. I watched as he worked his way up, shielding my eyes from falling bark. Once he was settled, he patted the empty spot next to him.

What did I get myself into? I groaned, slid over to the tree trunk and hugged it as I got to my feet. It was a little easier to get to him on the second branch since there was more to grab onto. That time, he didn't have to help pull me up.

"That was a little easier, right?"

"I don't think we should go any higher," I said nervously when I looked down and saw how far from the ground we were.

"Are you sure? We're *so* close." He pointed to the branch he'd originally suggested.

"Okay . . . but I don't want to climb any higher once we get there," I told him.

We both made it to the third branch and looked out through a small parting in the trees leaves. Everyone looked smaller from up there, but you could see all the way to the other parking lot from where we were sitting. I was glad I hadn't stopped at the second branch. We joked around and talked for a few hours as we played with the leaves around us. I learned that we had the same sense of humor, the same views on certain topics, and even the same favorite ice cream.

"I don't care what anyone says," Jules said after I'd asked. "Mint chocolate chip comes before vanilla bean, and vanilla bean comes before strawberry. All the other flavors will always try to be as good as them."

When we noticed it was early in the afternoon, we made our way back to the ground. He went first, all the way down, and waited for me as I followed slowly, in case I slipped. We made it out of the tree in one piece. He helped me fold the blanket, grabbed the bag of trash, and then we went back to my car. Once we were back in the campus parking lot, we got ready to go our separate ways. I didn't want to leave, but I had to go to work, so I didn't have a choice.

"Thanks for breakfast." I put the car in park and looked over to Jules. "And thanks for going with me to the park. It was nice to have some company for a few hours."

"Thank *you* for being so friendly to a complete stranger. I definitely enjoyed spending time with you. We covered quite a bit for two people that just met."

"You're right. I even climbed my first tree today." I blushed.

"It sucks that you have to go to work," he said. "I wouldn't mind spending more time with you."

"Yeah. There's always Monday, though. I *will* see you Monday, right?"

"Of course, you'll see me. I mean, I don't think we have the same classes other than algebra, but we can meet up in-between throughout the day, if that works for you."

On the inside, I was screaming and jumping around like a little girl who'd just gotten her first doll for Christmas. I hoped it wasn't obvious how excited I was. I managed to play it cool.

"Sure, that works for me."

"Great. I'll see you Monday."

I watched him as he got into his car. He made sure his mirrors were adjusted and then put his seatbelt on. Seconds later, he was waving to me as he pulled out of the parking lot. I waved back and waited until he was out of sight to do my happy dance—something I did when something really amazing happened.

When I got home after work, I told my parents about Jules over dinner. They hung on to every word I said until I was finished.

"Well, good for you, Marbles." My mother poured herself another glass of wine. "It's about time you met someone nice to spend time with. Is algebra the only class he has with you?"

"I think so." I poked at the food on my plate. "I didn't really get a good look at his schedule; I only took a glance at it."

"That's okay," my father said. "Maybe he's good at the subject, and he can help you study."

"Yeah, maybe . . ."

I hated that the weekend would probably drag, since I couldn't wait to see Jules again. I tried not to think about it, but after a few minutes of reviewing some class notes after dinner before heading off to bed, I couldn't help but go over the day again in my head. After a while, I took myself to bed so I wouldn't be tired for my morning shift.

Saturday morning flew by quicker than I anticipated. The customers that day were exceptionally nice and tipped well. I realized a few hours into my shift that we could have gotten a discount for breakfast if I had taken us to the diner I worked at instead of the one closer to the park. It was too late to change that, so I didn't dwell over it. I didn't want Jules to see where I worked anyway. It was a job, but it wasn't a job I was a hundred percent happy with. I wasn't sure what I wanted to major in at school, but I knew that once I decided on something, the job I'd get from it would be better than being a waitress.

Sunday evening, as I was getting ready to clock out, I received a text from Alora, asking if I'd be busy that night. I wasn't sure if I wanted to do anything with her, since I'd probably just end up hearing her complain about her relationship. Then I felt bad about having that thought and called to tell her I was free.

"Could you meet me at the beach in about an hour?" she asked.

"Sure," I responded flatly. "You'll *be* there, right?"

"Yes, yes, I'll be there," she answered quickly.

"See you in an hour, then."

I went home and changed out of my work clothes into some shorts and a T-shirt. After grabbing a quick bite to eat and letting my parents know where I was going, I headed out to meet up with her. Once I got there, I sat in the car for a bit, waiting for another car to arrive, since I was the only one there. After a few minutes, I got out and sat on the small wooden deck that looked out to the ocean. I was glad I got there before the sun completely set, since I didn't want to be out there alone in the dark. I checked my phone to see what time it was. *She should have been here by now. I'm only giving her thirty more minutes*, I thought.

An hour and a half passed, and she never arrived. I was seething at the fact that she'd stood me up. I didn't bother texting her to let her know I was there, and I didn't bother letting her know I was leaving. *She* had asked *me* to meet up with her. And she didn't even have the courtesy to let me know something had come up. She was just a no-show. I wasn't surprised, though, since it wasn't the first time she'd done that to me while dating Jordan.

Never again, I thought. I walked briskly back to my car and headed home. My parents were waiting up for me, watching TV in the front room. They could tell that I was upset the minute I walked through the door.

"Did she stand you up again, Marbles?" my father asked.

I nodded silently as I dropped my keys into a small bowl by the door.

"I *swear* that child has had one oar out of the water since she started dating that boy. You two used to be so close." My mother got up and went to the kitchen. I followed behind her, still not saying anything, with my father close behind me. "Don't worry, sweetie. She'll come around, I'm sure."

She poured me a cup of tea and set it in front of me as I got settled at the table. My father sat next to me and waited for a cup as well.

"As long as Jordan is in her life, she'll never come around," I grumbled. "She's too involved in his nonsense to see what she's destroying outside of what she *thinks* is a relationship." I took a sip of tea and held it in my mouth for a few seconds to savor the taste of chamomile.

"Have you ever thought of talking to her about it?" my father suggested. "I'm sure if you have a talk with her, she'll listen. At least then, if she doesn't seem to understand, no one can say you didn't try." My mother handed him his cup of tea as she took a seat across from us. "I'd just hate to see a friendship that you two have had for over a decade disappear over some boy."

"I'd talk to her, if I could ever get her to stay put. The last time I saw her was over the summer, and she gave me some excuse as to why she had to go. I couldn't hold her attention for more than two minutes. I just don't feel like trying anymore."

My parents looked at each other as I finished my tea and pushed the cup to the middle of the table.

"I'm going to bed. I'm sure tomorrow we'll have to make up the quiz we couldn't take on Friday. Night."

"Good-night, Marbles," they said simultaneously.

I thought about how I'd get to see Jules again as I got settled in my bed. If he was as genuine as he seemed, I wouldn't have to worry about him turning into a huge flake. He actually seemed to be a better friend than Alora had been over the last couple of years, and I'd only known him for a few hours. I took comfort in knowing that, after I went to sleep, I'd be waking up to a new day.

Chapter 10

I walked with extra pep in my step to my algebra class the next morning. Jules's car wasn't in the parking lot when I arrived, so I assumed he wasn't there yet. He still had about thirty minutes before he was late, so I didn't worry about it.

Once in class, I got settled in the middle of the room at the desk where I usually sat. There was an empty desk between me and another student, so I hoped Jules would sit there. Every time someone entered the room, I looked up from my notes, hoping to see him. For a few minutes, it was just a different student each time. At one point, it was the professor who arrived, leather briefcase in tow.

He started fumbling through its contents at his desk, as the room gradually filled. Before I knew it, it was time for class to start.

Where is he? I started to get a little anxious. *There's no way I read his class schedule wrong. It said that we have the same class. Maybe he decided to change it to a different day or time, since this one is early in the morning.*

Just as I finished that thought, Jules entered the room. He flashed a quick smile at me when he saw me. I smiled back, flooded with relief that he'd shown up.

"Mr. Reed, I presume?" the professor rasped. He still sounded a little sick.

"Yes, sir."

"You were cutting it pretty close, young man. Tardiness isn't tolerated in my class. Do I make myself clear?"

"Crystal."

The rest of the class grew silent as he quickly walked to the seat next to me and slid into the chair, quietly placing his books on the desk. He mouthed "good morning" to me as he took a mechanical pencil out of his pocket. I mouthed the same thing back, as the professor walked around and handed out the quizzes. Jules happily took his and started to fill out his name at the top. I was surprised that he didn't object to having to take it, since he was about three weeks behind, but I didn't say anything to him about it. Once the teacher got back to the front of the room, he told us we could begin.

I struggled through a few of the questions, but I figured I did well enough to get a passing grade. When I finished, I took the quiz up to the professor and placed it on top of the stack formed by students who had finished way before me. Apparently he was still feeling a little under the weather, so he was letting us go for the day when we finished. Jules was still working on his, so I waited outside the room for him. A few minutes later, he came out, carrying his books under his arm.

"How do you think you did?" he asked as we started walking to the end of the hallway.

"Okay, I guess. Math isn't really my strongest subject."

"I can always tutor you. And then maybe you can tutor me in a subject that I'm not very strong in. Sound good?"

"Sure does."

He held the door open for me as we made our way out to the courtyard where we'd first met. We got settled at an empty table and talked for a half an hour, until it was time to go to our next class.

"Where are you going next?" He asked.

"Basic Economics," I said.

"Oh. I've got Marine Biology."

He sounded a bit disappointed; maybe he'd hoped we would have another class together. I kind of felt bad for him, but I figured he'd be okay, since he seemed like the kind of person that everyone would like and want to talk to. "How was your weekend?" I asked him.

"It was okay. I picked up my textbooks and some school supplies. Other than that, it was pretty boring." He shrugged. "What about you? How was yours?"

"It was a weekend." I didn't say anything more than that. As much as I wanted to talk to someone other than my parents about my rocky friendship with Alora, it felt wrong. I figured if he wanted more details about my weekend, he'd ask.

I started to gather my books. "I've got to get going. How many classes do you have today?"

"Just the two," he answered.

"That sucks. I have three."

"I don't mind waiting for you after my biology class," he offered.

"Are you sure?"

"Yeah, it's not a problem. It'll allow me to walk around the campus to get the lay of it a little more, and help pass the time. Where's your economics class?"

I had a spare minute to write down the building and classroom number I'd be in. As I got up from the table, I handed him the piece of paper I ripped from my notebook, and then pointed in the general direction I'd be going.

"Great. I'll see you after my biology class."

We waved to each other as I headed to class. Even though the weekend wasn't all it was cracked up to be, I was glad the new week was off to a good start.

Chapter 11

Moments after Alex left, someone sat across from me. I looked over and was happy to find that it was James. He had the same biology book as me, along with a thin spiral notebook.

"Morning!" he chirped happily.

Without returning the greeting, I started telling him about Alex. I had only gotten to speak to him briefly after hanging out with her the Friday before. Now that I had his undivided attention, I made sure not to leave out any details. He listened intently without asking any questions.

Once I'd finished telling him everything, I was floating on cloud nine from a natural high.

"How crazy is it that she has a family nickname like I do? *Marbles.* It really fits her, you know?"

"I told you things would go smoothly. It wasn't that hard, now, was it?"

"Well, in the beginning it was a bit sketchy. But after a minute or two of talking, she started to loosen up a little."

"I'm happy for you. I wish I could interact with Alora, but the time isn't right. Instead I have to deal with beach visits on a regular basis." He sounded a little bitter about it, but I knew he meant well.

"You said the relationship she's in is coming to a breaking point. Be patient. You'll be able to talk to her soon."

"Yeah. Soon just feels like for*ever*." He groaned.

We hung out for a few more minutes, until it was time to make our way to class. We walked side-by-side through the courtyard and the hallways. I was glad I didn't have to try to find the class myself; I had gotten a bit turned around earlier that morning while trying to find my algebra class, which had almost caused me to be late.

The inside of the marine biology classroom was like the ones you see on TV. There were cabinets everywhere, jars with strange objects floating in them, lab tables for two to four students with stainless steel sinks in the center, a large lab table at the front of the class for the professor, and a huge blackboard on the wall. We walked in and took a seat in the center of the class next to each other. The professor was kind enough to go over the lesson from the week before, since it was my first day. I looked over James's notes, trying to copy down everything as quickly as I could. I heard him stifle a laugh.

"You *do* remember that I live above you, right?" he whispered. "You can always borrow my notes to look over or copy later. There's no rush."

"You're right."

Class seemed to end sooner than I'd imagined it would. I figured it'd drag, since I was eager to meet Alex at her economics class. I stood with James in the hallway as the other students were filing out slowly.

"Where are you off to now?" I asked.

"Home," he yawned. "I only take one class a day."

"That isn't going to slow you down or anything when it comes to graduating?"

"Not at all. The fewer classes I take, the less of a chance there is for me to run into Alora. Right now, I don't have any classes with her, and so far I rarely see her on campus. I'd like to keep it that way for the time being. Besides, I can always take a large course load over the summer if it comes down to it. Where are *you* headed?"

"I'm running to my car real quick to drop my books off so that I don't have to carry them around. I'm done with classes for the day. Then I'm meeting up with Alex so I can walk her to her last class."

"Okay. Give me a call when you're done here, so we can hang out for a bit. Remember: don't draw too much attention to yourself. That's how questions start. If you aren't prepared to answer them, you'll be backed into a corner and may risk compromising your situation."

"Trust me. I'm not here to make a bunch of friends outside of you and Alex. I know I have to be social to fit in and all, but befriending other people isn't my main concern."

"Good."

I nodded to James as we walked away in opposite directions. I made the mistake of going down the wrong hallway and got turned around unexpectedly while trying to find my way back to my car. It felt like it took me forever to find the parking lot it was in. After putting my books in the trunk, I briskly made my way into the courtyard as I pulled out my schedule to look at the campus map. The building and classroom number she'd written down matched the class I'd be taking on Tuesdays and Thursdays. I'd never noticed how all the buildings looked the same if you didn't pay attention to the numbers above the entrance doors or on the plaques affixed to brick walls on the side. *Pull yourself together*, I thought to myself. *Stay calm and focus. Finding this class shouldn't be difficult.*

I ran right smack into someone as I tucked the schedule back into my pocket. Books fell all over the ground, and I staggered backward. I realized I ran into a guy who was a little taller than I was. The girl he was walking with stared wide-eyed, and didn't say a word.

"Sorry," I said. I bent over to pick up the books I'd knocked out of the guy's hands, stacking them on top of each other while trying to make them look neat. "That was entirely my fault."

He watched as I made sure I got everything off the ground. I stood back up, and handed him his things. They both continued to stare at me as if I were from a different planet. I cleared my throat after a few seconds of silence, and cracked a nervous smile.

"What's your name?" the guy inquired.

It sounded as though he really didn't want to ask but did anyway. I eyed him for a second so I could decide what name I wanted to introduce myself under. It was a rule of thumb for me that only people I felt comfortable around could call me "Jules" or "Jax." Something about *him* put me on edge.

"Julian. And yours?"

"Jordan."

"Nice to meet you, Jordan."

I extended my hand to give him a handshake, but he eyed it and didn't move a muscle. I dropped it down to my side when it was obvious that he wasn't going to shake it. He didn't introduce the girl he was with. She was still standing by his side quietly, looking either to the ground or around at our surroundings. She was like an empty shell.

"Do me a favor, *Julian*, and watch where you're going from now on. I'm sure you're able to do that and read at the same time. It's called *multitasking*."

"Right. Sorry about that, again. I was just making sure . . ."

He didn't give me a chance to finish my sentence. Gently grabbing the girl's arm, he led her around me so they could make their way to wherever they were heading. I watched them as they disappeared into another building, still not speaking to each other as they walked. I made a mental note to steer clear of that couple in particular on campus. I broke into a light jog, hoping that I wasn't running too far behind. I didn't want Alex to think I wasn't showing up.

When I finally arrived at her class, I peered through a small window in the door to see if it was still in session. I was relieved to find that either the class had run over its usual end time, or that it was longer than I'd expected. It looked like everyone in the room was diligently taking notes from the blackboard. I watched as Alex checked her phone and shook her head as she started to write a little faster. She looked annoyed. I assumed it was because she was ready for class to be done and over with. When she looked up at the blackboard, she saw me at the door and flashed a quick smile. Her face brightened up when I smiled back.

I took a seat on a bench that was a few feet away from the door. About five minutes later, I rose to my feet when I heard the door open and saw students exiting the room. After a few of them walked out, Alex appeared and approached me quickly.

"I'm *so* glad that class is finally over. It felt like it went on forever. Today the professor just had us copy notes that he 'slaved over for hoooours,'" she mocked.

"Now *that's* funny." I chuckled. "May I?" I reached out and took her books from her.

"You really don't need to do that, Jules." She started to blush as she tried to hide her embarrassment. A few students were staring and whispering to each other. I wasn't sure if that was a good thing or not, until I remembered what James had told me about not drawing attention to myself. I didn't mind carrying her books for her, though, so I shrugged it off.

"It's no big deal," I said. "They're just books." I nudged her so she'd begin walking toward her last class. I didn't pay anyone in the hallway any mind as we made our way outside. We didn't have to walk very far before we arrived at her English Composition class. She seemed less flustered when we got there.

"Time for my most favorite subject of the day." She gently took her books away from me.

"Are you being sarcastic?"

"Not at all. This is honestly my favorite subject, I swear." She raised her right hand to show that she was telling the truth. "Thanks for carrying my books for me again."

"Anytime." I peeked through the window of the classroom and saw that it wasn't as full as her economics class or our algebra class. "I'm guessing this isn't a popular afternoon course?"

"Probably not." She said. "But the fewer people there are, the better it is for me. There's less noise and more one-on-one time with the professor."

"That makes sense. So . . . I can wait here for you, if you'd like."

"That's really nice of you to offer, Jules, but I have to head straight home after class to get ready for work. I wish I could hang out with you today. We should definitely plan to do something, though. I get my new work schedule tonight, so I'll let you know what the rest of my week looks like when I get home from work. Is that okay?"

I was a little disappointed. I had expected to be able to spend more time with her once classes were over for the day, but I understood that she had a job to go to. I didn't let it faze me.

"Sure, that's fine."

"Let me see that paper I wrote the economics room number on," she said.

I dug into my back pocket and handed her the crumpled piece of paper. She balanced her books the best she could, as she pulled a pen out of her purse. She scribbled her cell phone number under the building and classroom number she'd previously written and handed the paper back to me.

"Give me your number so I can give you a call or text you later," she said.

"Um . . . okay." I took the pen and one of her notebooks from her, trying to figure out what to write down. I had *no* idea what my cell phone number was. James had just given me the phone and told me that his own number was stored into it. I couldn't give her his number, and I couldn't make one up.

"Is everything okay?" Alex shifted her books from one arm to the other as she waited patiently.

Then it hit me.

I handed the pen and notebook back to her and pulled my phone out my pocket. I quickly composed a text and sent it to her so the number would show up on her phone. That way, she could save it to her contact list later.

"That was a good idea." She dropped the pen back into her purse and zipped it closed.

We said our goodbyes as she walked into the classroom. I made my way back to my car, placing her number into my wallet for safekeeping. There was no way I would have been able to explain not knowing my own phone number. I needed to sit down and think of explanations for anything and everything that might come off as suspicious.

Chapter 12

Once I was in the car, I called James to find out where he was. He told me he was at the beach, so I didn't hesitate to make my way there. I wanted to tell him about the couple I bumped into on campus and about the phone incident with Alex. When I arrived, I parked next to James's car and made my way up the wooden steps that led to where he told me he'd be. Looking around after getting to the small wooden deck, I discovered that no one was out on the beach. I was confused for a second, but then I heard someone below the deck.

"Down here."

I looked over the wooden railing. "James? What're you doing down there?" I watched as he parted some of the grass to reveal his face.

"Is there anyone out on the beach?" he asked.

I looked out again to be sure before answering. "No, no one's out there. Are you hiding from someone?"

He approached the side of the deck and climbed up, scanning the beach as I had done to double-check before climbing all the way up. After getting over the railing, we made our way down to the beach. We walked parallel to the ocean for a few minutes before he stopped and sat down in the sand next to a large, bright-colored shell. He picked it up and chucked it into the ocean and then started digging in the sand slowly. He pulled a folded piece of paper out of the hole and read over it quietly as I took a seat next to him. When he was finished, he filled the hole with sand and shoved what he'd read into his back pocket.

"Sorry, what did you ask me back there?" he asked as he got more settled.

"I asked you if you were hiding from someone. I think I already have my answer."

"I wasn't *hiding*, per se. I got here, thinking that Alora had already come and gone, but she showed up a little after I arrived. I dipped under the deck so she wouldn't see me."

"I think that's considered hiding, James." I laughed.

"You make it sound creepy, though."

"Those shells you chuck away: is that how you know where she buried something?"

"That, or I look for small sand mounds left behind from when she fills the holes back in. But I can't always depend on those, since anyone could have made them."

After talking about what he'd read, we headed to the diner by the park to grab some lunch. He listened as I told him about my unpleasant encounter with the couple on my way to Alex's economics class. I could tell by the look on his face that the incident didn't sit well with him. I hoped that once I got to my *real* dilemma about giving answers to personal questions, he'd be more interested in trying to help me with that. Unfortunately, it was painfully obvious that he was still stuck on the courtyard incident.

Our food arrived after I'd finished telling him everything that happened that day, and we ate in silence. I patiently waited for him to say something as he coasted through a cheesesteak sandwich and some fries. I poked around at my baked potato, since the silence was starting to concern me. After James finished all the food on his plate and took a few sips of soda, he finally spoke.

"This guy from campus . . . what'd he look like?"

I looked up from my food and thought about it. There was nothing about Jordan specifically that I could remember—other than the look on his face when I gave him his books and the fact that he was a little taller than me.

"Nothing stood out about him, really. He's smug though, I can tell you that. He didn't even shake my hand when I offered it to him." I pushed my plate away. "He also didn't introduce the person he was with. She looked like a lost puppy. She didn't say a word the entire time we were in the courtyard."

"*She*? He was *with* someone?"

"Yeah. They were walking together to class I guess. If I had heard them coming toward me, I would have moved out of the way. I was too focused on the campus map, trying to find Alex's class."

"Did you happen to catch his name?"

I couldn't tell if it was excitement in James's eyes or a hint of anger. The last thing I wanted was for him to go looking for this person to find out what his problem was, so I played it safe. "I didn't, sorry."

He eyed me from across the table as he tried to figure out if I was lying. Apparently, I was convincing enough. He slouched heavily in the diner booth and massaged his right temple slowly. He was obviously frustrated but quickly apologized for his reaction. "I'm sorry. I'm not upset with you. This definitely wasn't your fault. Accidents happen. You should have been more careful, but accidents happen."

"I definitely plan on making an effort not to run into either of them on campus again. That guy looked like bad news."

"He probably is."

James paid for both our meals again, and I thanked him profusely. I couldn't wait until I could start working so I could have my own money. I didn't want him always to come out of pocket for me.

That evening, I sat at the dining room table and copied some of James's biology notes he'd loaned to me. I was eagerly waiting for a call or text from Alex to let me know what her work schedule was going to be for the week. After realizing that it was getting late, remembering that I had an early economics class the next morning, I cut off all the lights and went to bed. I kept the phone close, in case she called or texted me before I fell asleep. Once my head hit the pillow, though, I was dead asleep.

Chapter 13

It was unreasonably busy at work. All I wanted to do was to go home and text Jules to tell him I'd be busy after school until Saturday. Someone called in sick when I was ready to head out the door that evening, so the shift manager begged me to stay and help close. I didn't mind working a few extra hours, so I agreed.

I was busy wiping down tables and collecting dirty dishes when I heard someone walk into the diner. I didn't look up from what I was doing, hoping they weren't coming in to sit down to eat. That would have meant I'd have to stay even longer. Luckily, they were ordering food to go. The voice of the person placing the order sounded familiar.

I looked over to the front counter to discover that it was Alora and her boyfriend Jordan. She was standing close to him, resting her head on his shoulder. He didn't show any PDA back. I rolled my eyes and went back to what I was doing.

It was just my luck that she looked around the diner and saw me wiping down the tables for the night. She left Jordan's side to come over and talk to me. I just wanted her to go away and leave me alone. I was still angry at her from the night before.

"Hey, Alex," she said quietly.

I grabbed the two glasses sitting on the tabletop and pushed by her, placing them gently in the rubber bin so I could take them to the kitchen. She moved to the side when I walked back over to the table to continue spraying and wiping it down.

"I'm really sorry about last night," she said. "I got caught up and lost track of time. I should have called to tell you."

"But you *didn't*." I pushed by her again to grab the rubber bin, making my way to the last table that needed cleaning.

"I *should* have, though. I know I keep bailing out on you after asking if you're available."

"Listen, Alora, I'm trying to clean up so I can go home. You should know that your apologies don't mean anything to me at this point."

"You know I mean it when I say I'm sorry. I'm not doing any of this on purpose."

"I don't know the difference between what you're doing intentionally or unintentionally anymore. I just know that I'm tired of trying to figure it out."

I quickly wiped down the last table, pushed the dirty plates into the bin without caring if they broke or not, and snatched it up. She followed close behind me as I made my way to the front of the diner. Jordan was checking through their bag to make sure everything was there. *Good, now they can leave*, I thought.

"I'm just trying to make things right between us, Alexia. *Please*, just give me a chance to try and fix things," Alora pleaded. She grabbed my arm, and I shrugged her away as Jordan approached us.

I gave a curt nod in his general direction. "Get rid of your baggage. Then we can talk."

I didn't look back as I made my way into the kitchen. Jordan mumbled something under his breath, and they left without saying another word to me. It took everything in me to not go running after her so I could tell her how I felt: that I wanted her to leave him because he was no good for her. I just wanted things to go back to the way they had been before he came into the picture. But I knew it'd go in one ear and out the other. The dishwasher took the bin from me, and I went to the back of the diner to grab my things from my small locker in the manager's office. After jotting down my schedule for the week, I clocked out, and left for the night.

Unexpected traffic caused me to get home later than I'd planned. I didn't even have time to look through my biology notes for the next day. When I checked the time and saw how late it was, I didn't think it would be appropriate to contact Jules. I figured I'd find him on campus the next morning and tell him when I'd be free to hang out with him again. *Hopefully he doesn't think I forgot about him, since I didn't call or text tonight. I'll just explain how crazy it was at work when I see him.*

Chapter 14

When I woke up the next morning, it felt as though I hadn't slept for days. I kept checking my phone throughout the night, hoping to find a missed call or text from Alex. After a while, I came to the conclusion that she'd either forgotten or gotten busy. I remembered that she had gone to work after her last class, so I just assumed it was the latter and that we'd talk when I got to school. James dropped by while I was eating breakfast. We hadn't gotten around to discussing my other dilemma, the one I thought was more important, while we were at the diner the day before.

"Worst case scenario," James advised, "you answer any questions you get asked about yourself with another question. That'll give you time to figure out an answer to what you were asked originally. And make sure your answer is something you can remember, in case you're asked the same thing by a different person."

"Got it."

"You're sure? I don't mind hanging around with you on campus until you're used to being around large groups of people again." He took a sip of the juice I'd offered him when he arrived and eyed my economics and literature textbooks on the table between us.

"I should be okay now," I said with a mouth full of cereal. "Yesterday I just got a little tongue-tied. You don't have to worry about me."

"Well, you know I'm just a call away if you need me, right?"

"Yes, Dad," I shot back sarcastically after having another spoonful of cereal.

"I'm serious, Julian. You're making some amazing progress with Alexia, and it's only been a couple of days. I'd hate for something to happen that causes you to have to go back, you know?"

The fact that he didn't call me Jules told me he was serious. I hadn't meant to joke with him about it, so I apologized and reassured him that I'd be fine. Satisfied with what I'd told him, James nodded, and pulled out his wallet. He slid forty dollars across the table and waited for me to take it.

"James . . . ," I began.

"I don't mind helping you, and I don't expect you to pay me back. You never know when you might need a little cash handy."

I reluctantly took the money and put it in my shirt pocket for safe keeping until I could put it in my wallet. "Thanks." I drank the rest of my juice and started to clear the table. "I promise I'll find some way to repay you."

"Trust me. Having someone to talk to on a daily basis is enough of a repayment. Don't stress it."

James helped me clean up before leaving. He said he'd catch up with me at school, since we'd be in different classes. "I'll wait by your car when I get out of class." He dried his hands on a dish towel and placed it on the kitchen counter. "How many do you have today?"

"Two: Basic Economics and then World Literature."

"I'll see you after your economics class then."

After making sure everything was secure in my apartment, I grabbed my books from the table and headed to campus, eager to meet up with Alex. I couldn't wait to see her again and to find out what her work schedule was for the week.

When I got to my usual parking spot under the willow tree, Alex's car wasn't there, but James's was. I waited for a few minutes but then decided I'd try to find her after class, since I didn't want to be late. I didn't have a hard time finding my first class of the day, since I'd already walked Alex to the same room the day before. When I got there, the students that were already seated grew quiet as I found a seat in the middle of the room and faced front. After a few seconds, they went back to talking quietly. No one approached me, which was a relief. I'd told James that I had everything under control when it came to being social, but I was still a little worried that I'd screw up, one way or another.

I was happy when the professor arrived and class finally began. We pretty much had to do the same thing Alex had done the day before. We all tried to keep up with the professor as he wrote notes he'd "slaved over for hours" on the large blackboard. I laughed to myself when he said that. Alex's impersonation of him was spot-on.

Once I'd finished copying everything he had written into my notebook, I let him check my work and was released from class. On my way to the car to swap out my books, I checked my phone to see if I'd received anything from Alex. I eagerly opened a text message that she'd sent sometime that morning and learned that she wanted to meet up with me in the courtyard after class. I quickened my pace after shoving the phone back into my pocket.

James was sitting on the hood of his car as he patiently waited for me. Alex was parked on the other side of me, but she wasn't there.

"Is that Alexia's car?" James asked.

"Yeah," I answered quickly.

He slid off his car and walked over to hers to check out the front of it. He eyed the license plate thoughtfully, touching it with the toe of his shoe. "It's a bit plain, don't you think?"

"What's plain?"

"Her car. It needs something."

"I guess," I shrugged. "I never really looked at it in that sense. A car is a car to me."

"How was economics?" He came to the trunk of my car as I dropped the text and notebook I'd used for that class into it.

"Boring." I quickly grabbed a different notebook and the textbook I'd need for World Literature.

"Someone's in a hurry." He rested against the side of my car and waited for me to close the trunk.

"Alex texted me while I was in class. She wants me to meet her in the courtyard."

According to James, I looked like a child that had just received a shiny, red toy fire truck for Christmas. He walked with me to the courtyard and left me there to wait for her alone. He was going home so he could work on sketches for some license plates and plate frames he'd need to make at work later that week. I sat at an empty table and flipped through a few short stories in the textbook, trying to answer some of the comprehension questions at the end. *I* hate *this subject*, I thought. *Maybe Alex can help me with it.*

I nearly jumped out of my seat when someone grabbed my shoulders from behind and shouted at me.

"Morning!" Alex laughed as she took a seat next to me.

"You scared me!" I took a deep breath, trying to stop my heart from beating so fast.

"I couldn't resist. Sorry I didn't call you or anything last night. Things were crazy at the diner, and I got home late."

"That's okay."

"Now, about this week . . . I'll be pretty busy with work and everything, but we can plan something for Saturday since I'll be off. We can still meet up between classes until then, but I won't be able to hang out the way we did last Friday."

"That'll work," I said. Everything was coming together better than I'd thought it would. "Did you have anything in mind that you wanted to do?"

She poked at my school books as she thought about it. I noticed that she only had her purse with her and remembered that she'd only had biology that morning. *She must have gone to her car a little after James and I had left the parking lot.*

"I'll let you decide on something," she said. "Anything *you* want to do, I'll be more than happy to do with you."

"I'll make sure to think of something fun. How was class this morning?"

"Eh, I'm not a big fan of microbiology, but it's better than algebra. How was yours?"

"I have the same economics class you were in yesterday, so we had to copy notes. It was a pretty boring first day for that one. Is the professor always so—I don't know—disconnected from the class?"

Alex shook her head. "I don't think so. I've found that he gets flustered every couple of days and doesn't put much effort into working from the syllabus he gave us last week. We don't complain, though, since we don't have to do much of anything but write the entire time, and we get out early afterward."

I checked the time on my phone and saw that I needed to head to class. Alex leaned in to give me a hug and said she'd talk to me later. I was happy that she was comfortable enough with me to show that kind of affection. I told her to have a good day at work. She said she would try and that if she didn't get home too late she'd shoot me a text that evening. Once she was out of sight, I went to my last class for the day.

My literature class was more crowded than the other classes I had attended so far. The only seat available when I got there was in the back next to one other empty seat. I wasn't too fond of sitting anywhere other than the middle of the room, so I figured I'd try to get there earlier the next time to get a better seat. Just as the professor was about to start her lecture, the girl who had been with Jordan the day before walked in. She hesitated when she realized there was only one seat left. My heart sank a little as she reluctantly made her way to the back to sit by me.

I didn't make eye contact with her as she got settled and the professor began. For a few minutes, it was as if she wasn't sitting next to me. I wasn't sure if she was reluctant to sit there because she recognized me from the day before, or if it was because her usual seat was taken. I *did* notice that she looked extremely tired and, if I was right, upset. I watched her with my peripheral vision as she played with her pen lazily, trying to keep her head up because she was falling asleep. It looked like she was writing a letter to someone. The formatting looked familiar, and so did her handwriting. Trying not to look suspicious, I turned my head just a little to see if I could get a better look. After a minute or two of not being able to make out what she was writing, I started leafing through my textbook.

"I'm sorry about yesterday," she whispered, slipping the paper she was writing on into her notebook and opening her textbook.

I turned the page, not sure if she was talking to me or not.

"You're Julian, right?" She kept looking in her textbook and not at me. I guessed that she was trying to talk to me without the professor noticing.

"Yeah," I whispered back.

"I'm sorry about yesterday, Julian. My boyfriend can be a bit . . . rude."

"It's not a problem. I should have been watching where I was going."

"He could have watched where you were going too and moved out the way, but he was being a prick. So I'm apologizing for him."

I nodded as we both turned the page in our books simultaneously. I wasn't even reading what was written in it; I was just trying to keep up with appearances. The class went by slowly after she spoke to me. I wanted to get away from her so there wouldn't be any problems with Jordan later.

"Are you new around here?" she asked.

Everything in me screamed to pretend that I didn't hear her question, but I knew that I shouldn't be that way toward her. In all reality, she wasn't the one I wanted to avoid; it was her boyfriend. The fact that she had apologized for him made her seem pretty harmless.

"Yeah, I moved here a little over a week ago."

"From where?"

"California."

"I heard it's nice over there."

"It is, depending on where you live."

"Did you want to share something with the class, Mr. Reed?"

I hadn't realized that the professor had made her way to the back of the room and was standing in front of our desks. The girl next to me continued to read and didn't say anything. I'd gotten caught, since I was the last one to speak.

"No."

"Then could you please refrain from having personal conversations while class is in session? These students have paid good money to enroll in this course, and it's rude of you to make their learning experience less than enjoyable because you're talking to your friend while I'm trying to teach."

"Yes, I'm sorry."

After she'd walked away and started her lecture again, the girl next to me tapped on her desk lightly to get my attention. She'd managed to scribble a note on a used sheet of paper while the professor was standing there. She slid it to the edge of her desk for me to read: *Don't mind her. She's not always like that, and she usually doesn't mind a little bit of talking during class. My name is Alora, by the way.*

I stared blankly at the note. This was *Alora*? Once I knew who I was sitting next to, everything made sense. You could see that her relationship with Jordan was taking an emotional toll on her. There wasn't anything I could do to help her with her situation. And since James couldn't do anything either until the time was right, I figured it wouldn't hurt to get acquainted with her—in case she needed someone to talk to.

"Nice to meet you, Alora," I whispered as quietly as I could.

She smiled and went back to reading her textbook. *Hopefully, this won't be considered interference,* I thought. *I just won't tell James about it.*

Chapter 15

Meeting Jules between classes during the week went smoother than I'd expected. After he got a hang of where his classes were and how much time he had in-between, we didn't miss a beat when it came to getting together to talk for a while. We even started texting each other around the same time every night, until it was time to get some sleep for school the next day. He was turning out to be someone I was slowly beginning to confide in.

While he claimed he couldn't stand his literature class, he was picking up on it faster than I thought he would. He needed little to no help—the way I needed help with algebra. I figured maybe he just thought the worst when he saw what was in his textbook. His comprehension when it came to certain short stories was amazing; I admired it. I wished I could have said the same when it came to me understanding algebra. He always found a way to squeeze in a bit of tutoring, even though we never had a lot of time for it before we had to go our separate ways.

"I'll never get the order of these equations right," I groaned on Wednesday as I dropped my pencil in frustration.

"Sure you will." He picked the pencil up and put it back into my hand. "Once you get the hang of 'PEMDAS,' you'll be okay; trust me."

Friday arrived before we knew it. Thanks to a minor schedule change, I had some extra time before I had to go to work that day. When I told Jules, he agreed to meet up with me at the park after he'd put some gas in his car. I waited for him at our usual hangout spot under the willow tree after placing my blanket on the ground. There weren't many people out there, so it was pretty quiet. All you could hear were the birds chirping in distant trees and the occasional insect buzzing by. When he arrived, he had a couple of Slurpees with him and some sour candy. He had remembered that they were my favorite and had grabbed a bag before leaving the gas station.

"Aw, thanks, Jules." I took one of the cherry Slurpees and the candy, as he sat down next to me.

"Don't mention it."

We sipped on the cherry goodness while staring out at the lake.

"I'm glad you ended up with a little extra time today to hang out," Jules said after taking a long sip from the plastic cup. "I wish we had more time like last Friday, though."

"We'll have all day tomorrow." I reminded him as I offered him some candy. He placed his hands out, and I shook a few pieces into them. "Did you come up with anything for us to do?"

"Not yet."

"Well, when do you *think* you'll come up with something?"

He popped a piece of candy in his mouth. I could tell by the look on his face that he was trying to hide how sour it was. I leaned over and looked him in the eye, popping a piece of candy in my mouth as well. My face didn't screw up in the slightest like his did, so I wanted to show how much tougher my taste buds were. He laughed, then drank some of the Slurpee and held it in his mouth. After a few seconds, he swallowed everything.

"I'll be sure to have a plan by the time you get off work."

His phone rang. I zoned out as he took the call, so it wouldn't seem like I was listening in on his conversation. He wrapped up the call quickly and got to his feet.

"That was James. I have to go."

He seemed a little flustered, which was a first. I hadn't seen him show any emotion other than his overall happy and laid-back demeanor, so it made me a little curious—and concerned.

"Is everything all right?"

"He said he needed to talk to me. He sounds a little pissed off, so I should go see what's wrong."

"Okay. I'll talk to you later then?"

"Yeah. By then I'll have something planned for tomorrow, don't worry."

After helping me fold the blanket, we walked back to the parking lot. He finished the rest of his Slurpee on the way and tossed the empty cup into the trash. I gave him a handful of candy for the road. He thanked me and quickly got into his car. "Text me when you get off work, okay?"

I nodded as he quickly drove off, leaving a small cloud of dust behind.

From there I went home to change. My mother talked to me from the doorway of my bedroom as I dressed for work.

"How was your day?" She sipped on some tea as I looked around for my apron.

"I got to hang out with Jules for a bit at the park after class, but that got cut short, which kind of sucked."

"Is everything okay?"

"He said his friend sounded upset, so he needed to go and see what was wrong."

"Oh, don't worry. I'm sure if it were something extreme, you'd know. What're you looking for, Marbles?"

"My apron. I can't go to work without it."

She walked away from the doorway as I started looking under the pillows on my bed. When she came back, she was holding my apron up for me to look at it. She had washed it for me while I was at school and stitched my name on the front pocket in black so I wouldn't have to wear my name tag. I walked up to her and gently took it.

"Thanks, Mom." I put it on, and she tied the back for me.

"Get to work before you're late." She led me to the front door and handed me my purse. "We'll see you when you get home."

Chapter 16

I pulled into a parking spot next to James's car and jogged up to his apartment, knocking quietly on his door when I got to the third floor. I waited patiently for him to answer. Once he let me in, we both walked to the couch and took a seat.

"What's up?" I asked.

"Did you happen to catch the guy's name that you bumped into on Monday?"

My heart jumped into my throat. The look on his face told me that there was no way I could lie to him again about not knowing Jordan's name.

"I figured, since you said that you *didn't*, that I'd just ask someone else," he said flatly. "Did you *seriously* think I wouldn't find out?"

His voice raised a little, but I stood my ground.

"Okay, yes, I lied to you about that. I'm sorry I did, but I'm kind of *not* sorry at the same time. If you could have seen the look on your face when I told you I bumped into him, you would've lied to you too."

"What else have you been keeping from me? You might as well come clean about *everything*, since I might already know."

I hadn't told him that I had literature with Alora on Tuesdays and Thursdays. In just two days, I had gotten to know her pretty well. I didn't think that my talking to her in class would affect her regular routine of writing letters and lists and then going to the beach to bury them. At least from what she was saying, it didn't. James hadn't reported a change in her beach visits that week either, so I figured what I was doing was acceptable.

"I've got a class with Alora two days a week. I've been getting to know her since Tuesday. But that's it, I swear. I didn't mention you or anything. She's been volunteering information."

James stared blankly at me. I couldn't tell if he was about to explode into a fit of rage or if he was processing what I'd just told him.

"What have you found out about her?"

"Outside of the fact that she's *really* unhappy in her relationship and that she visits the beach to bury letters and lists, nothing."

"Has she told you when she's going to the beach?"

"On Tuesday she told me that she was going that day and Wednesday. She didn't say anything about it yesterday. Would it help if I told you everything she says about her visits? She apologized about Jordan's behavior in the courtyard on Monday. After I learned who she was, I honestly wasn't sure what to do when she continued to hold a conversation with me."

James got up and went to the kitchen. When he came back, he offered me a bottle of root beer with the top already popped off. I took it from him and took a large drink from it.

"That *would* help," James said. "I'd be less stressed out. She's been getting a little sporadic with her beach visits lately, with everything that's going on between her and Jordan. Is that all you need to tell me?"

"Yes. I think she just needs someone to talk to who's willing to listen. I don't think she has many friends. If I find out anything that may help you, I swear I'll tell you."

James took a drink of his root beer. "Thanks. You know I wasn't upset with you, right? I'm just frustrated with her situation . . . and a little jealous that you get to talk to her." He sighed. "I can't see myself ever getting mad at you, unless you did something directly to me."

"I don't want to step on anyone's toes—especially yours. I should have told you what was going on, though. Wait, how'd you find out that I knew Jordan's name?"

"Security cameras, my friend. I asked one of the campus security guards if I could see the tape from that day. I have connections on and off campus."

"Oh, you're crafty."

"I wouldn't call it that. I just know how to use my resources." He smirked.

Once that water was under the bridge, I told him about my other classes outside of the one we shared on Mondays since we didn't get to talk much all week. As it got later in the evening, I remembered that Alex would be texting soon to find out about Saturday. I still had nothing to suggest.

"The only thing I've been coming up with is the park. We've already spent time together there twice, so I don't want to suggest that again."

James took our empty bottles into the kitchen and placed them into the sink. I watched him rinse them out as I stood at the counter close to the front door.

"Well, the flea market is open tomorrow, and I'll be working. I didn't go today because I've been sketching designs to fill some online orders. You can take her there, if she's into that sort of thing. You've been to one before, right?"

"I used to go a lot with my parents back home." Memories flashed before me, as I remembered how we'd go looking for faux plants and area rugs for our house. We'd always made it a point to buy funnel cakes and hotdogs while we were there.

"Well, I think going there would work for the both of you. I can make a license plate frame for her car, if you'd like."

"That sounds like a good idea. Did you have a design in mind?"

"Maybe. I've been working on something for *your* car since you arrived last Sunday. It'll be ready tomorrow. You said her family nickname is *Marbles*, right?

"Right."

"Hmm . . . I'll come up with something for her; don't worry. Do you remember how to get there?"

"I'm sure I do. You think she'll know if I *don't* remember?"

"I hope so."

I received a text from Alex, asking about Saturday. "She just got off work." I stared at the phone, trying to figure out what to write back. "I'm not sure what to say, exactly."

"Tell her you have to go to the flea market because you need to pick something up. Ask her if she'd like to join you for the day."

I keyed the text the same way James had put it and sent it to her. As I waited anxiously for a response from her, he slid me another root beer. After a few sips, I received a response.

"Well? What did she say?"

"She said it sounds like fun, and she'll see me tomorrow morning at the park."

"Then I'll see you both at *Plates & Frames R Us* tomorrow."

Chapter 17

I arrived fifteen minutes early at the park to meet up with Jules. I was so excited to hang out with him for the day that I was too antsy to sit in the house after getting dressed. When I saw him pull into the parking lot, I checked my hair in the rearview mirror, and waited to get out my car until he parked next to me.

"This was a great idea." I closed my car door and adjusted my purse on my arm as I watched him walk around the front of his car. "It's been a while since I've been to the flea market."

"I figured it'd give us a chance to walk and talk so we can get to know each other better—outside of helping one another with context clues and math expressions."

"I grow weary of math expressions," I frowned.

"Well, we don't have to worry about them. Not until Monday, at least." He opened the passenger door for me, and I slid into his car. Although it wasn't brand new, it *smelled* brand new. I inhaled the scent as I put my seatbelt on. He got into the car and got settled.

"So outside of walking and talking, what's this thing you have to pick up while we're there?" I asked as I watched him put his seatbelt on.

"A custom license plate frame. It's supposed to be ready today, so we'll have to make a quick stop at that booth."

"I've been looking for something like that for my car. I wasn't able to find anything that really grabbed my attention, so I gave up looking about a year or two ago." It was difficult for me to find anything marble-themed when it came to car accessories. It was probably because Marbles wasn't a common nickname.

"Today may be your lucky day, then," Jules said. It looked as though he was trying to hide a smile as he pulled out of the parking lot. I figured it was because he was excited about the day ahead of us, so I didn't give it a second thought.

We laughed and joked as he took his time driving to our destination. It was nice to know that he had the same sense of humor and active imagination as me. It helped when it came to telling the most random and off-the-wall stories.

"Wait," Jules began, "you're saying he met with an Eskimo in Antarctica, and they both spent the day ice fishing with a yeti . . . and his traveling partner is a *camel*?" He chuckled as we sat at one of the many red lights we encountered.

"According to Benny, that's what he did," I said. Benny was someone I'd made up a few years ago as a joke. But after a while he had kind of turned into a "real" person that only *I* heard from when it came to his world travels. Most of the time, I used him as an excuse for why something was misplaced at home. Occasionally, I'd share his amazing adventures with people for entertainment purposes. For the most part, it always had positive results.

Although it seemed like we hit every red light on the way, it felt like no time before we were backing into a parking spot in the oversized parking lot. Jules had shifted the car's gears flawlessly the entire ride there. I had trouble singing aloud and writing at the same time, so the fact that he was able to shift gears and keep a conversation going without stalling out amazed me. *I need to learn how to drive stick shift*, I thought. *He makes it look so easy.*

We both unbuckled our seatbelts after he turned the car off.

"I bet today we can find you something for your car," Jules challenged.

I glanced over at him. "I told you, I haven't been able to find anything marble-related. I can't even find seat or steering wheel covers. I'll end up empty-handed again today, just like I did the last time I bothered looking."

He made a face that showed he really didn't believe me. "You just weren't looking in the right place, that's all. This is a *flea market*, a place where you can find fancy and unique trinkets, including some pretty cool junk. You know what they say about junk." He pushed his seat back so he could put his wallet into his pocket.

"One man's junk, is another man's treasure." I smiled.

"That's the spirit. Now, let's do some treasure hunting."

After getting out of the car, he waited for me in front of it, while I carefully stepped out onto the loose gravel of the parking lot. I'd made a split-second decision that morning while getting dressed to wear a pair of my favorite wedge shoes. I didn't want to lose my footing; I had done that one too many times in the past in front of complete strangers, even while wearing regular sneakers.

Before taking any steps, I made sure I had my balance. I walked around to the front of the car where Jules was waiting, but I still managed to lose my footing a bit while trying to step as carefully as I could. My face scrunched up as I looked up to him to see if he saw the slight stumble. He smiled, and offered me his arm. I didn't hesitate to take it, embarrassed that I needed help walking like I was a little kid.

"That wasn't the best choice of footwear for today, huh?" he chuckled.

"I guess not."

He bumped me playfully as we walked slowly toward the entrance. After a few steps, once he was sure I had a good enough grip on his arm in case I stumbled again, he put his hands into his pockets.

Once inside, we stopped and gazed at all the booths that were readily visible. Whenever I visited the flea market, I always made it a point to look over the layout when I first walked in. That way, I could trace my steps back to the original entrance I'd come in from. There were at least twenty aisles to go down. After a while, if you didn't pay attention to where you were going, they all started looking the same. And once they started looking the same, you ended up going in circles rather than ending up at your original starting point. One day it took me an hour to get back to my car. After *that* incident, I knew that I needed to take note of the things I passed periodically, so I wouldn't get turned around again.

After we checked the map to find the location of the booth that Jules was looking for, we walked side-by-side down one of the many aisles. We talked and laughed the entire time, as we poked around in different booths as we made our way there. It felt as though we'd never run out of things to talk about, which was a plus. I usually ran out of things to discuss with people, especially if I had just met them. But with Jules, I felt like I could talk to him for hours on end about anything, and he would willingly listen and give his insight.

An hour after stop-and-go walking and talking, we finally made it to *Plates & Frames R Us*, an oversized booth where customized license plates and license plate frames were made. I didn't remember seeing it there before, but then I remembered that it had been over a year since I'd been to the flea market.

Jules made his way to the checkout counter located toward the back, gazing at the many pre-made plate designs hanging on a wall on the way. I broke away from his side and began browsing through what looked to be hundreds of design booklets lying on a wooden table. Jules started a conversation with a guy who appeared behind the counter before he'd made it all the way to the back. They were talking as if they had known each other for years.

I came across what looked to be a one-paged pink booklet with letters sprawled all over the cover that was resting at the end of the table. I gazed toward the back of the booth and saw Jules viewing a wall of blank plates and frames that were ready to be custom designed. The guy behind the counter was gone, so I assumed he went to grab Jules's order.

I slowly reached over and grabbed the pink booklet, not expecting anything out of the ordinary when I opened it. I had assumed it would contain a single page with different font choices, since there were letters all over the cover, but I was surprised at what I saw.

"Find something?"

I looked behind me to find Jules looking over my shoulder.

"I think so," I said with a hint of excitement.

He took the book out of my hands, looked the picture over, and nodded in agreement. "I think so too. It has 'Marbles' written all over it."

He was right; it literally had marbles all over it. The rough sketch of the frame design had multicolored cat's-eye marbles all along the sides and my family nickname, Marbles, was engraved at the bottom center of it in script. It was almost as if it had been custom-made for me. I gently took the book back from him and gazed at it dreamily.

"It's beautiful." I said, trying to hide my disappointment.

"What's wrong?" He stooped over, placed his chin on my shoulder, and continued to look at the picture in the booklet with me.

"The detailing is amazing. I can only imagine how much work would have to be put into this. It'd probably be on the pricey side to have it made—*well* over twenty-five dollars. I don't have that kind of money right now. I don't get paid for another week, and I've got more important things to pay for first. I wish I could get it today, though. Maybe in a few weeks."

I shut the booklet and placed it back on the table. I had a feeling that if I didn't get it that day, the design probably wouldn't be there when I came back. It was always my luck that when I found something I really liked, it was gone without a trace if I took my eyes off it for just a day.

"I'm sure there's something we can work out with the booth clerk," he said.

Without saying another word, he picked up the booklet, gently took me by the arm, and led me to the counter.

Chapter 18

After pulling me forward so I was walking next to him, he let go of my arm and wrapped his around my shoulders. "But, Jules, I don't have money for this right now," I mumbled. "I'm sure it'll be here next week . . . or the week after that if I'm lucky."

"Come on. Would it hurt to see if it's even available?" he insisted. "It won't do anyone any harm to ask."

Once we got to the counter, Jules pressed a small button on the countertop that caused a buzzing sound to echo through the booth. We heard someone in the back push away some boxes and put down some tools.

"Be right out!" a voice called.

It only took a few seconds for someone to appear—the same guy that Jules had talked to when we'd first arrived. He wore a large smile on his face as he wiped his hands clean on the black apron tied around his waist.

"I was putting some finishing touches on your frame. I want to make sure it's perfect before you walk out of here with it."

Jules slid the booklet across the counter. "You wouldn't happen to have this frame in the back, would you?"

The booth clerk looked at it closely, stroked his chin, and then looked back at Jules. "As a matter of fact I do. There's *one* available."

"One, huh?" Jules said. "How convenient. What made you think to make something like this?"

"Dunno. It just struck me as something that'd put a smile on the face of someone who goes by the name of Marbles."

I stared blankly at the clerk as his smile grew larger. *How'd he know?* I looked at Jules and saw the same smile he had tried to hide when we first left the park to make our way there.

"Alexia," Jules began, "I'd like to introduce you to James. He's the friend that lives above me. James, this is Alexia."

James came from behind the counter to greet me.

"You can call me Alex," I said. I extended my hand for him to shake it, but instead he took it lightly, placed one foot forward, and lowered his body slightly by bending at the knees. It took everything in me not to laugh right in his face. "Did you just *curtsey?*"

"It's a pleasure to finally meet you." James stood up straight and let go of my hand. "I've heard so much about you."

"James has an amazing sense of humor," Jules pointed out. "He can be quite the character."

"Clearly."

James went back around the counter and put the booklet under it to make sure it didn't go back on the table with the others. Jules leaned on the counter and got comfortable, as I placed my purse between us.

"I'm glad you found this place okay. I was worried you got turned around on the way, especially since it took you so long to get here." James pulled out a signature book for Jules to sign, showing that he had picked up both the frames.

"We walked around for a bit when we arrived." Jules quickly scribbled his name on both the dotted lines. "I figured it'd give you more time to have everything ready." He slid the book and pen back to James, who placed it under the counter with the booklet he'd stashed away.

"You were in on this, weren't you?" I asked Jules.

"Kind of." He smirked.

James went to retrieve the frames. We stood in silence and waited for him to come back. The day was turning out to be better than I'd thought it would be. When he returned to the counter, he had two plastic bags in his hand.

"Here's the frame that I made special for you, Jules. And here's yours, ma'am." He gingerly handed them across the counter.

Jules took them both, handing mine to me. "Thanks again, James. It was enough for you to make mine, just because. You went above and beyond to make one for Alex too. I owe you one."

"Hey, I'm putting my talents to use, so it's not a big deal or anything. I thought she'd like it. And her car was looking a little plain, so I figured it'd make a great addition."

"What're you doing later?" Jules asked him.

"I'll be at home. I have more designs to sketch for tomorrow, so that's where I'll be if you want to stop by."

"I'll call you when I'm on my way, then."

They shook hands as I grabbed my purse off the counter to leave.

"Thank you for the frame, James," I said to him. "It was nice to meet you. I hope we see each other again soon."

"No problem—and likewise."

When we stepped out of the booth, we took a moment to look in our bags at our newly acquired items. My frame sparkled in the overhead lights, causing the colors on the marbles to show on the inside of the white plastic bag. I closed it and peered over into Jules's to look at his. His family nickname, Jax, was engraved in bold block lettering at the bottom center of it, with a small halo over the letter *a*. After the quick inspection, we both began to walk the crowded aisles toward the entrance we'd come in, so we could get back to his car.

Jules lightly placed his hand on my lower back as we turned a corner and had me walk in front of him. The crowd seemed to have gotten thicker since we'd first arrived. Walking single file was always best when it got busy, and it was courteous to the other people shopping there. We took our time, as we went down a few more aisles, to look at antiques and paintings. We even managed to grab a funnel cake. I laughed as he took a mouthful of the treat and ended up coughing out a cloud of powdered sugar.

"You're supposed to chew it, not inhale it." I popped a small piece in my mouth as I walked away from him and the ordering window.

"I got a little ahead of myself," he said. He caught up to me and handed me another piece.

When we got back to the parking lot, I looked at the time on my phone and saw that the day was still young. It felt as if the whole day had passed, but then I remembered that we'd met at the park fairly early that morning, had taken our time getting there, and then had walked around some before and after getting the license plate frames. After throwing away the empty paper plate and cleaning our hands, I took hold of Jules's arm before he could offer it and walked next to him back to his car. He didn't object to it; he actually seemed happy that I'd taken it on my own.

"What should we do now?" he asked, kicking a rock off to the side.

"I'm still a little hungry. The funnel cake was just a snack, really."

"Well, where would you like to eat?"

He didn't seem bothered with my need to feed. But when I thought about it, why would he be? I was hungry, and he probably was too. Now it was just a matter of not suggesting anywhere too expensive, or too cheap.

"Is there anywhere *you* would like to eat?" I asked him, unsure if my vague suggestion was a good one. It was obvious that it had impressed him.

"I like that: someone who's open to accepting suggestions instead of always making them. How about we eat at the diner you work at?"

I stopped walking and let go of his arm as he knelt down and stuck his hand under the front bumper of his car. Seconds later, he was holding a screwdriver that he must have placed there for emergencies. He took each screw out of the plastic frame already around his license plate, slipped the new frame around it, and put the screws back in to keep it in place. Then he put the screwdriver back under the car.

"How'd you know I worked at a diner?" I peeked into my bag again, admiring the colors of the cat's-eye marbles. Suddenly my stomach growled. I hoped that he hadn't heard it, as I gently rubbed it and waited for an answer.

"Remember the first day we met and I walked you to your car?"

"Yeah." I thought about it and I figured out how he knew, without further explanation. I sometimes placed my uniform and apron in the trunk with my books so I could head straight to work after school. He had known all along where I worked but had never said anything. "Well, that makes sense," I said.

"So, it's okay to eat there? I can understand if you don't want to eat where you work. Especially since you're off."

"It's fine. I can get an employee discount. I just didn't want you knowing where I worked, that's all."

"Why? It's a job. It's better than nothing, right?"

"True. But it's just not where I want to be."

"Well, I'm sure in time you'll have the job of your dreams. For now, it helps make ends meet. I don't think less of you because of where you work."

"Really?"

He laughed as he walked to the passenger door and opened it for me. After I got in, he walked around and got in himself. Once he was strapped in, he started the car. "I'd only think less of you if you told me you were a world-class thief or a serial killer."

"Benny does that."

"Which one: steal or kill people?" he asked with a raised brow.

"He steals! Shame on you for thinking he'd kill anyone."

"Benny is a world-class thief, too?" He said with a hint of skepticism.

"Sure. He and his camel travel to different countries to steal precious stones locked away in temples and palaces."

"He'd be better off with a cat as his sidekick for *that* kind of thievery." He put the car in first gear and pulled out of the parking lot.

"A cat?"

"Yeah, you know. A cat. Which would make it a cat burglar."

I shook my head, happy that he was able to roll with the story. I directed him to the diner where I worked, as we continued to make up stories, letting them get to the point where we were laughing so hard we were in tears.

Chapter 19

My coworkers made sure they brought our lunch to us quickly after we sat down and placed our orders. Knowing Jules didn't judge me because of where I worked was a huge relief. I sometimes forgot that it wasn't as big of a deal as I sometimes made it out to be. A job was a job; there were people who couldn't find work.

"Did you need anything else, Alex?" our waiter asked.

"No, everything is fine for now, thanks." I took another bite of the bacon cheeseburger I'd ordered.

"Julian?"

"I'm fine too, thanks."

The waiter quickly left so we could be alone again. Business was slow that afternoon, so he found himself stopping by our table more often than he usually would have, to make sure everything was okay.

"This diner is *much* better than the one we went to for breakfast last week." Jules cut into the chicken he ordered, giving it time to cool before trying to eat it.

"I figured the other place was the best choice because it's closer to the park. That, and I didn't want you knowing where I worked at the time."

"You shouldn't feel any less than awesome because of where you work. If anything, you should ignore anyone who has an issue with it for whatever reason."

"I'm working on that." I put more ketchup on my plate so I could finish my fries.

"Alex," the waiter began as he approached our table again, "a couple just walked in and recognized you." He said. "They want to know if it's okay to join you."

I looked toward the front of the diner and saw Matt and Sam waving excitedly at me. For a second, I was afraid I'd see Alora and Jordan instead.

"Sure they can. You don't mind, do you, Jules?"

"Not at all. Scoot your plate over so I can sit next to you," he said.

The waiter went to get them, as we rearranged everything on the table so they could sit across from us. By the time they got to our table, the other side of it was cleared for them.

"It's *so* good to see you, Alex!" said Sam. "I feel like it's been forever since we've talked." She and Matt both slid into the booth and got comfortable.

"Julian," I said, "this is Matt and Samantha. Matt and Samantha, this is Julian."

Matt was the first to shake Jules hand; Sam was second.

"You can call me Sam." She grabbed a menu and started looking through it.

"And you two can call me Jules. It's a pleasure to meet you both."

When they were finished with the food they'd ordered, we sat and talked for a few hours. They took to Jules as if they had known him for as long as the three of us knew each other. We asked the waiter to bring our bills when we were ready to leave.

"Thanks for letting us join you for lunch," Sam said. "We would have understood if you two wanted to eat alone. I'm glad we were able to catch up." She finished her soda and placed the cup on the table.

"I've been meaning to get together with you guys for a while now," I admitted. "I just didn't want to be the third wheel."

"You shouldn't feel that way, Alex," Matt insisted. "I mean, I know you wouldn't want to tag along with us *all* the time when we're together, but we're always here if you just want to talk or hang out for a bit."

"Yeah, we're not like Alora and Jordan," Sam chimed in. "We still want to keep up with you so we know how you're doing."

I thought I felt Jules stiffen up when Sam said their names. When I looked at him, he seemed okay, so I figured it was just me.

"Have you heard from her at all?" Sam asked.

"She wanted me to meet her at the beach last Sunday," I said, "but she stood me up. Then they came here Monday night to order takeout food. She tried to talk to me then, but I blew her off. I kind of felt bad afterward."

"Why? You didn't do anything. *She* did. She's supposed to be your best friend. Instead, she's treating you and everyone else like we have a disease."

Matt took their check from the waiter when he approached. I took our check, only to have Jules take it from me.

"I'll get it," he offered.

"Are you sure?"

"Yeah, it's no big deal." He took out his wallet and started leafing through the money inside of it.

"I know she's been acting off since she started dating Jordan, but that doesn't mean I should act the same way toward her," I continued.

"Personally, I think any way you act toward *either* of them is deserved at this point," Sam puffed. "Who abandons everyone that's ever been there for them—for a guy who thinks he's the best thing since sweet tea?"

"Sweet tea?" Matt interrupted.

"Yeah."

"I don't think that's how the saying goes, Sam."

"If that's not how it goes, then what's the right way of saying it?"

I shook my head thoughtfully as they playfully squabbled over something so trivial. It was obvious that they were happy with where they were in their relationship. They were able to have disagreements and still be able to laugh about it afterward without holding a grudge against each other.

After paying for our meals, we walked out to the parking lot so we could go our separate ways. We stood out there a few minutes more to wrap up our conversation.

"Have you had the pleasure of meeting the lovely couple in question, Jules?" Matt opened the car door for Sam. She got in and sat with the door open so she could still talk to us. Jules looked as though he was trying to come up with an answer.

"I, uh, I met Jordan earlier this week."

"You didn't tell me about that." I waited for him to continue.

He shrugged. "I didn't think I needed to. I ran into him when I was on my way to meet up with you at your economics class on Monday. He didn't say much, and I've made it a point to avoid him ever since."

"What about Alora? Have you met her?" Sam questioned.

"I have literature with her on Tuesdays and Thursdays. She seems nice."

"She only seems nice because she's finally found someone that's actually willing to listen to her problems." I scowled.

For a moment, we all fell silent. At that point, I was just ready to drop the subject. I wasn't mad at anyone; I just didn't want to talk about it anymore.

"Okay, well, we've got a movie to catch in about an hour so we need to get going," Matt said. "It was nice meeting you, Jules. Hopefully, we'll see more of you around—the *both* of you."

After shaking Jules's hand good-bye, he and Sam left to head to the theater. Jules opened the passenger door for me and then went around and got into the car himself. Both of us sat quietly. I wasn't sure what to do next. I just knew I wanted to get my mind off Alora. Without saying a word, he drove us back to the park.

Chapter 20

We ended up sitting at our usual hangout spot under our favorite tree once we got back to the park. The sky was starting to turn a cotton-candy pink as the sun slowly set. We hadn't spoken to each other the entire ride there, which had me feeling a little ill at ease. He didn't seem angry when I looked at him as we made our way up the hill to the tree. His face was expressionless as he watched his footing on the damp grass. He didn't offer his arm to help me walk because of my shoes, but he didn't shrug me off when I took it on my own. Once we were under the tree, we spread out the blanket and got comfortable next to each other to watch the sky change colors as it got darker. All the while, neither of us said a word.

Fireflies started to appear after a few more minutes of silence. He watched as a couple of them floated by, his face still expressionless as one landed on his hand. He let it walk around in circles before gently brushing it off so it could be on its way.

"Did you have fun today?" he asked. He had finally broken the silence. There was no emotion in his voice, and he still stared at the sky as he waited for me to answer.

"Yes, today was great. I'm glad I got to meet James. He seems really nice. And it was good to see Matt and Sam again. I haven't spoken to them in a while, so it was nice to find out how they're doing."

"Good. I'm glad you enjoyed the day. And I'm glad I got to meet some of your friends." He brushed a firefly off his hand again and blew another out his face. There seemed to be a large number of them out that evening. We tried not to let them bother us too much.

"Alora is your best friend?" he asked abruptly.

"If that's what you'd like to call her." I crossed my legs out in front of me and slouched a bit.

"How long has it been like this between you two?"

"I'd rather not talk about it." I was trying to stop the conversation before it went any further, but it was obvious that he had thought a lot about what was said at the diner.

"I think you *should* talk about it."

"Why? If I said I don't want to talk about Alora, then I *don't* want to talk about Alora. And besides, I've only known you for what, a week? So it's no business of yours what's going on between me and her anyway."

"Do you hear yourself right now? I bet, if you could, you'd spit nails when you say her name. I only want to understand what's going on. Maybe I can help."

"You can't help someone who doesn't want to be helped. We've tried that—me, Matt, and Sam. We've tried telling her that Jordan was changing her and that she wasn't the same person we've known for years. I've tried meeting up with her when she asked me to, and she's only stood me up. Then, the next day, she comes up to me, apologizing. I don't even know what *sorry* means anymore, because she's abused the word so much. *Sorry* doesn't mean anything when there's no sincerity behind it."

"How do you know she's not being sincere?"

"If she were, she wouldn't keep hurting her 'best friend.' *That's* how I know."

I could feel myself about to cry, but I didn't want to. Jules scooted closer to me, so our arms were touching, and crossed his legs out in front of him as well.

"Keep going; get it all out," he said.

"I don't want to," I pouted.

"I bet you'll feel a hell of a lot better if you do," he coaxed.

My parents were amazing listeners, but they still didn't understand. They would always tell me that Alora would come around, but for me, that wasn't good enough. Matt and Sam could tell me until they were blue in the face that they'd always be there if I needed someone to talk to, but I still wouldn't seek them out for anything. Since college had started, all I wanted was someone I could talk to and know that everything I said would be kept between us, and help me sort things out when I couldn't.

Then I'd met Jules, someone who seemed more loyal and genuine than most people I had known. Even after I'd gotten a little nasty with him, he *still* wanted to listen to me.

"I'm sorry I said this was none of your business." I sniffled.

"It's okay. You're just upset."

"'Upset' is an understatement."

I told him everything—from how at first Alora would still hang out when she started dating Jordan, up to when she started slacking on her friendship responsibilities. It had been going on for a little over two years, but it felt like an eternity. I managed to talk about all of it without dropping a single tear, and when I was finished, it felt like I'd gotten *so* much off my chest. The entire time, he didn't say a word. He let me talk or shout about whatever was bothering me, without even flinching.

When he knew I was finished, he put his arm around my shoulders and gave me a one-armed hug as hard as he could. "I know we've only met a little over a week ago, and we don't really know each other *that* well, but I'm definitely glad I met you. Know why?"

I shook my head.

"Back home, I felt the same way as you with a few of my friends. But I learned that sometimes people grow apart as they get older, and there isn't much we can do about it but sit back and hope for the best. I'm not saying that you two will never get back what you had, but this is something you have to let her go through. She'll either realize what's happening, or she won't. I can relate, so you're *not* alone.

I'm glad I met you, because I can help you the same way I was helped when I needed it for this sort of thing. I can't replace Alora, but I can be there for you until she comes back around."

I wrapped my arms around him and hugged him back.

"Even if she *does* come back around, I hope you won't disappear on me."

"Nah, at this point I think it's safe to assume you're stuck with me. I already know too much." He laughed.

We sat and stargazed for a little while longer until we mutually agreed it was getting late. I had to be to work the next morning, and he'd told James he'd swing by that evening. I gave him another hug before we went our separate ways.

"Thanks again for today. I'll put the license plate frame on my car tomorrow before I go to work."

"Don't mention it. I look forward to hanging out with you like this more often."

"Text you when I get off work tomorrow?"

"Sure. I'll be looking for it."

When I got home I showed my parents what I'd gotten from the flea market. My father held it up to the light in the kitchen and ran his finger over the engravings. The colors of the marbles danced and flickered on his face.

"This is some *amazing* craftsmanship. Julian made this for you?"

"No, his friend James works at one of the booths there. He made it."

"It's very nice. Want me to put it on the car for you?"

"It can wait until tomorrow, Dad. There's no rush."

He placed it back in the bag and handed it to me.

"Sounds like you had a good day." My mother dried the last plate in the sink and set it on the counter.

"Oh, it was great! We poked around some of the other booths while we were there and grabbed some lunch at my job. He even got to meet Matt and Sam."

"I haven't heard about them in a while. How're they doing?"

"From what they told us, they're doing pretty good."

"I'm happy that they still come around every so often to check in with you. I just wish Alora would do the same thing." She said, shaking her head while folding the dish towel.

"Well, as we grow older, we start to grow apart a little. So all I can do is stand back and hope for the best. She'll either realize what she's doing, or she won't. Her situation is out of my control."

"That's a good way to look at it, Marbles." My father sounded impressed.

"Jules gave me a pep talk before I came home."

"He sounds like a smart young man. Will we get to meet him at some point?"

"Sure. Once I get to know him better, I'll be sure to bring him by."

After talking to them about my day, I headed off to bed so I would be well rested for work. I couldn't predict the future, but I had a good feeling that the relationship I was developing with Jules would only get stronger over time.

Chapter 21

After leaving from the park, I headed straight to James's place. *I wonder if he knew that there was a connection between Alex and Alora but didn't tell me.* I didn't bother calling him when I was on my way like I'd said I would. After parking next to his car, I trotted up the stairs and knocked on the door. It didn't take him long to let me in and invite me to sit at the dining room table. He was cooking dinner, so he put a plate down in front of me, along with some utensils and a glass filled with ice cubes. Whatever he was making smelled amazing.

"Alex really liked the frame, huh?" He stirred what was in the pot on the stove with a long wooden spoon while sprinkling in some salt.

"Of course. It was exactly what she'd been looking for. Thanks again for making it for her on such short notice. I hope it didn't set you back or anything."

"It didn't. Anything to help. You know that."

He brought one of the pots over to the table and took the lid off. Using the large wooden spoon, he scooped out some spaghetti, dropped it in the center of my plate, and then served himself some. Afterward, he brought over the second pot, which contained the sauce with slices of Italian sausage in it. He poured it over the spaghetti until he felt that there was enough spread over all of it. He then gave himself some sauce and went back into the kitchen to leave it on the stove. Once he'd tidied up a bit, he brought over a pitcher of juice and poured me a glass.

As we ate, he told me about the rest of his day at work. He'd had a few customers come in after Alex and I left, but other than that, business was slow. That gave him time to work on a few orders that had come in via the Internet, so he could ship them off when they were finished. After we finished eating, he took the plates and put them in the dishwasher. I was stuffed and could feel myself getting tired. That's when I remembered the conversation I'd had with Alex and her friends at the diner.

"Did you know that Alex and Alora are friends?"

James dried his hands after getting the dishwasher going. Once he was sure that the kitchen was clean, he came back to the table and sat across from me.

"No. Are you sure we're talking about the same Alora?"

"Yeah. I met two of her friends today while we were having lunch. Apparently, the four of them used to hang out—until the two I met today started dating each other, and Alora started dating Jordan. Ever since then, the three of them have been having a hard time keeping up with Alora, because she's been blowing them off."

"Well, you read just about all the letters and lists she writes and buries at the beach. She didn't mention any of them. That's crazy though."

"Right? I convinced Alex to vent about it to so I could get a better understanding of their relationship. It's not doing well. Jordan is really driving a wedge between the both of them. She's not happy about it."

"Well, there isn't anything *we* can do to help. That's between them, so they're both pretty much on their own."

"If anything, getting Alex to talk about it brought us a little closer. I think she knows she can confide in me."

"And that's a great start. I'm sure as time passes, you two will be thick as thieves."

That night as I drifted off to sleep, I thought about how things had been going since I'd returned to the world of the living. It had only been a little over two weeks, but I was making some amazing progress. If everything went well, it was possible that a tight-knit group would form. I tried not to get too far ahead of myself, though, since I had just met Matt and Sam that day, and because anything could happen with Alex as we got to know each other better.

There was also the fact that James still had to wait for Alora's situation to change before he could do anything. The thought of the six of us becoming close friends felt amazing, though. And knowing that there was a strong chance at Alex and I being "thick as thieves," felt even better.

Chapter 22

After that Saturday, the two of us were inseparable, spending more time with each other between and after classes and whenever I had time off work. I liked that my daily routine had changed. I had Jules to thank for that. As time passed, I got to get to know James better as well. The three of us would sometimes meet up in the courtyard or go out on the weekends to catch a movie or to hang out at the beach. We also managed to squeeze in a couple of double dates with Matt and Sam. I found that the more time I spent with Jules, the more confident I was getting. I wasn't second-guessing myself about things I normally overanalyzed, and I was a lot less cautious over the little things I'd used to fret about.

Before we knew it, the fall semester was coming to a close. One Thursday afternoon, I decided to surprise Jules while waiting for him to show up at the park. I watched from a branch in the willow as he walked up the hill with a bag full of snacks. It was hard to stop myself from giggling as he got closer to where we would sit on the ground before climbing into the tree after eating. I looked on as he slowed his pace, and gazed down to the lake and then back down to our cars. The look of confusion on his face was priceless.

After looking down at the lake and back to the cars a second time, he pulled out his phone. Mine started to ring as he placed his to his ear. He looked up into the tree when he heard the custom tone I'd made for him coming from my phone. I waved to him when he saw me.

"I see someone got over her fear of heights and climbing trees alone." He laughed.

"I thought I'd surprise you." I started to make my way down, but he told me to stay put.

"We can eat up there. There isn't much in the bag, so we'll be okay."

Once he reached the branch I was sitting on, we ate all the snacks he'd brought up with him. We talked about school for a bit and about my job. I asked him if he'd found one yet, but he wasn't having much luck.

"You could always work with James at the flea market on the weekends. He seems to be doing well for himself there."

"That's a good idea. I don't know why I didn't think of that myself. Why are you so smart, Miss Waters?" He said with a deep southern drawl, which made me laugh loudly.

"I get it from my ma and pa, sir," I said as I began to swing my legs lazily.

"You're off work tonight, right?"

"Indeed I am. Why? Did you want to do something?"

"As a matter of fact, I do. You like seafood?"

"Yeah, but we don't have to go anywhere fancy. I know you're not working and everything."

"I wouldn't offer if I couldn't afford to treat. And it's nowhere fancy; it's got a pretty laidback atmosphere. That being said, I'd like to take you out to dinner tonight. How's that sound?"

"Like a plan. Will it be just us, or will we be having company?"

"Just us. James has to look over some sketches for work, and Matt and Sam have plans themselves tonight."

After hanging out in the tree for a couple more hours, we both headed home so we could get ready for dinner. I wanted to make sure I was ready on time for when he came to pick me up. My parents had met him a couple of weeks after we went to the flea market. As far as I could tell, they adored him.

"Going out tonight with Julian?" my father asked. Both he and my mother were standing in the doorway of my bedroom, watching as I sprayed on some perfume and put on a belt.

"Yup. We're going to a seafood restaurant."

"Do you know which one?"

"Well, I think there's only one in town, and that's the one with the faux ship on shore out back. At least I think it's faux. Do you think it's faux?"

"Probably, Marbles. I wouldn't put too much thought into it."

The three of us looked out my bedroom window when we heard the doorbell ring. I checked the time. Jules was early. Whenever he was picking me up to go somewhere, he was *always* early. My father loved that. He went to let Jules in so he could talk to him for a few minutes while I finished getting ready.

"You won't be out too late, right?" My mother inquired.

"I doubt it. We've got that final exam for algebra tomorrow morning. We'll be back at a reasonable time."

"Okay, good."

After I kicked on a clean pair of sneakers, making sure the bottom of my jeans rested neatly over them, I walked out to the front room. Jules and my father were sitting on the couch, laughing about some joke that was in the newspaper that morning.

"Did you get the joke, Julian?" My father laughed as he tried to catch his breath. "It took me a minute to get it myself, but when I did, I nearly cried."

"I did, Mr. Waters. It was definitely hilarious. Your delivery was on point, too." Jules smiled as he got up from the couch so we could leave. "You know, you and Mrs. Waters can call me Jules." He insisted.

"Thank you Julian, but we feel more comfortable calling you by your full name." My father patted him on the shoulder as he followed him to the door. "Don't stay out too late. You've got that final tomorrow."

"Don't worry, we won't," I promised.

My parents closed the front door behind us as we made our way to his car. "I told them that we were going to the local seafood joint with the faux ship in the back. That's where we're going, right?" I asked.

"That's the only seafood restaurant I know of." He opened the passenger door for me, and I got in.

"Have I told you how awesome you are lately?" I smiled up at him as I started to put on my seatbelt before he shut the door.

"You haven't; but then again, you don't have to. If I *weren't* awesome, I'm sure you wouldn't bother spending all this time with me."

Once he was settled in the car himself, we made our way to the restaurant. While sitting at a red light, I watched as he shifted the gears while waiting for it to turn green.

"You know, I don't know how to drive stick shift," I pointed out.

"Really? It's pretty easy to learn. I can teach you when you're ready." He shifted to first gear and accelerated after the light finally changed.

"I'm ready to learn when you're ready to teach."

"When's the next time you're off?" He pulled into the gravel parking lot of the seafood restaurant and parked in front of a large log that was a few feet away from the front door.

"Not for a few days, but I get off early on Saturday."

"Saturday it is. You should get the hang of it after an hour, tops."

We walked arm-in-arm up the steps into the restaurant. It was kind of packed, but the wait time wasn't too long. We waited patiently outside for someone to come get us when a table was available. After about five minutes of cracking jokes and holding small talk, I heard familiar voices exiting the restaurant. I took a quick glance at the doors, and my stomach sank.

It was Alora and Jordan.

Jules obviously didn't see them when they passed by, as he continued to try to tell me the joke my father had told him before we left my house. I was hoping that they wouldn't see us, but unfortunately, Jordan noticed Jules and stopped just as he and Alora began to make their way down the steps. He turned to look back at both of us, and a mischievous grin appeared slowly on his face.

"Well, look who's here," Jordan scoffed. "Alexia and Justin."

"It's *Julian*," Jules corrected.

"My mistake," he sneered. "Knocked any books out of the hands of unsuspecting passersby lately, or have you learned to walk and read at the same time?"

"It wouldn't have happened if you would've moved out of the way yourself," I cut in. "And that happened months ago. Why are you bringing it up again?"

"This doesn't concern you," he shot back.

"Don't you have anything better to do than to bully people you don't even know?" I could feel myself getting angry, as I tried to control the volume of my voice. I didn't want to draw attention to the four of us.

"I didn't know Jeremy needed a bodyguard."

"It's Julian," Jules reiterated calmly.

"Right. My apologies again, Julius."

"Come on, Jordan. Let's just go. There's no reason to start any trouble. We're having such a nice night." Alora tried to talk Jordan into walking away, but he didn't budge.

"Oh, what? You're standing up for your friend now? I can leave you with these two pushovers, if that's what you want, and you can find your own way home."

"I'm not standing up for anyone. I'm just saying that there's no reason to cause any problems when we're having such a nice night."

Great way to stand up for yourself and your friend, you coward, I thought.

Jordan stared at her coldly for a brief moment. She cleared her throat and looked away as she grabbed him gently by the arm. "Nice seeing you, Alex. See you for the final next week, Julian."

"You have a *class* with this guy?" Jordan hissed as she tried to pull him down the rest of the steps.

"You'd know that if you actually listened to her instead of keeping her muzzled like she's a yappy little dog." Jules pointed out.

"Are you trying to tell me how to work my relationship?"

"From what I can see, you don't 'work' anything but your oversized ego, when in reality you're just as empty and insecure as you make *her* feel," Jules shot back as he pointed at Alora.

Jordan snatched his arm out of Alora's hand and started to approach Jules. Just as I stood between them to prevent anything from going any further, a large man stepped out of the restaurant and grabbed Jordan by the shoulder.

"Is there a problem here, Jules?" the man asked gruffly as he pushed Jordan back toward the steps without much effort.

"No, sir. They were just leaving. See you in class next week, Alora. Night, Jordan."

Jordan looked at both of us and then up at the large man who still had him by the shoulder. He shrugged him off as he stormed down the steps with Alora right behind him. We watched as they got into his car and sped off toward her apartment complex. I waited until they were out of sight to start breathing again. I'd been almost positive there was going to be a fight between the two of them, right there in front of the restaurant. I was glad someone else had intervened; I wasn't sure if I would have been able to stop it once it started.

"Your table is ready, Jules. Take a minute to collect yourselves. Someone will take you to it when you're ready." He patted Jules on the shoulder, and Jules nodded to him as he went back inside.

"Who was that?" I asked.

"He's the owner of the restaurant. James introduced me to him the second or third time we came here for lunch. He's a real nice guy."

"Nice is an understatement." I said. "He came out here just in time."

"You okay?"

"I'm fine. I can't believe that just happened. I didn't know Jordan was so confrontational."

"Well, now we know."

We stared out into the parking lot for another minute or so before going inside to eat.

"Don't let what happened ruin our night." Jules nudged my arm with his. "She'll be okay after all that, though, right?"

"Who, Alora? She'll be fine."

"You're sure?"

"If you're worrying about what I *think* you're worried about, don't. He's very arrogant, but he's not stupid. He'd never hurt her like that."

"You're sure?" he asked again.

"Positive."

"Okay. You didn't have to step between us, you know."

"I know. It's not something I'd normally do; I try to avoid confrontations at any and all costs. But this time, I felt the need to take action. I'm actually kind of proud of myself." I smirked.

"We make a good team, obviously." He laughed. "Come on. I don't know about you, but that whole ordeal really worked up an appetite."

Chapter 23

We ended up sitting in one of the best booths in the restaurant, which was located by one of the many large windows. We had an amazing view of the inlet that was behind the restaurant. The raw clams on a half shell that I'd ordered a few minutes after we were seated arrived quicker than I'd expected. I took my time dressing each one with lemon juice and horseradish. Jules watched as I prepared all twelve of them without saying a word—until I actually got ready to eat one.

"You're not *really* going to eat that, are you?" Jules asked. He tried to suppress a shudder, as I picked one of them up.

I paused before slurping up the cold, lifeless seafood, and laughed at the look of despair written all over his face. "Of course I am. Why wouldn't I?" I brought it to my mouth, ready to take in the raw goodness, when he asked another question, causing me to pause again just before the cold clam touched my lips.

"Are they good?" He poked with a salad fork from across the table at one that was lying on my dinner plate.

"Don't do that. You'll make the lemon juice spill out." I lightly swatted his fork away. "And yes, they're good. If they weren't, I wouldn't have ordered them." I quietly ate the clam, chewing it happily, knowing it would make his skin crawl. I watched as his face went all in a twist as I swallowed it.

"It just looks gross," he commented.

"Hey, don't judge me, or the clams, sir."

Within a matter of minutes, I was finished eating all twelve. I took a sip of my soda after setting the last clam shell onto the plate of melting ice, and watched as the waiter approached with Jules's meal. I almost gagged at the smell of his entrée, as I set my glass back down on the table. His eyes danced as he took the rest of the silverware out of the crisp, white napkin they were wrapped in.

"*You're* not going to eat *that*, are you?" I questioned in the same tone he'd used when asking me about my meal. He began to slowly cut what was on his plate into small pieces.

"It's fried eel," he said. "I like fried eel." He separated the pieces into a straight line so he could eat them one-by-one.

"How can you poke fun at *my* food, when you're about to eat what smells worse than what *I* ate?"

"Hey, don't judge me, or the fried eel, ma'am," he said with a crooked smile.

"Ha ha, smart-ass." I turned up my nose and gazed out the window into the distance. Jules moved from cutting up his food to drenching it with tartar sauce, lemon juice, and pepper. I was glad that our orders had arrived separately. We usually ate at the same time, but it was probably a good idea to not have the two different dishes at the table together—especially when we were equally grossed out by what the other had ordered.

I watched as the water from the inlet lapped the side of the large ship that had been strategically placed on shore for patrons to gaze at while they waited for their orders to arrive. I often wondered if there was anything in it that would be worth seeing—like a treasure chest under the deck of the ship or maybe even treasure maps. Light from the rising moon was shining through the thin clouds onto the tattered sails, making it seem almost as if it were ready to set sail under invisible command.

"Want to try a piece?"

I turned to answer him, finding a fork full of dripping eel inches away from my nose. I sat back quickly and shook my head.

"Ewlk. Thanks, but no thanks."

"Okay, but you don't know what you're missing." Jules stuffed the food into his mouth and chewed happily.

To avoid getting sick from watching what seemed to be an endless amount of eel disappear, I went back to looking out the window until it was obvious that he was finished. He took the napkin the utensils had been wrapped in and wiped away crumbs of food from the corners of his mouth.

"What's up? You're not still thinking about what happened earlier are you?" Jules inquired.

"I'm wondering if there's anything inside that ship out there." I turned away from the window once again and looked at Jules. "What if there's a treasure chest inside that no one knows about? A treasure chest filled with old coins and trinkets worth a lot of money?" I could feel my eyes grow as large as silver dollars, as I let my imagination soar.

"I'm not sure if this kind of thinking is any better than dwelling on the death match that almost occurred when we first got here. You're letting your imagination get the best of you." He chuckled. "Anyway, I doubt there's anything in there. I'm sure it's just a prop the owner placed there, meant purely for entertainment purposes. At least, that's what James told me." Jules took both of our plates and stacked them on top of each other in the middle of the table.

"But *we* don't know that for sure, right?" I pointed out, while making quotation marks in the air with my fingers to emphasize the word *we*. "*We* don't know if it was put there for entertainment purposes—or if it's a genuine ship that shipwrecked years ago with something of great value on it." I grabbed my glass and finished the soda that was getting flat from the melting ice. "*We* know nothing about it."

"*I* know plenty," Jules said, "except about *you*. *I* don't know about *you* anymore. *You* 'sound' and 'look' crazy, throwing finger quotations around like they're gang signs." He mimicked me while making a goofy face.

"Shut up," I said, laughing.

"So, what're you suggesting, since *we* know nothing about that ship? That *we* take a look *ourselves*?" He took out his wallet and leafed through the cash he had. The waiter came by, scooped up the plates, and dropped the bill on the table.

"What else do we have to do tonight? I mean, we've got that final exam tomorrow, but it won't take us hours to check the ship out. The night's still young."

I slid out of the booth and watched as Jules dropped fifty dollars on the table after he looked at our bill. He didn't respond as we walked to the front of the restaurant side-by-side. We waved to the owner on the way out. Jules grabbed a couple of mints from the podium by the entrance, handing me one as we walked out the double doors. I continued speaking a million miles a minute, trying to convince him that looking inside the ship was an amazing idea. He listened intently until I asked for his opinion.

"I don't know," he said. "A lot could go wrong with this crazy idea of yours. Did you think about that?" He began to slowly make his way to the wooden steps that led down to the gravel parking lot.

"Well," I began, popping the green mint into my mouth, "the worst that could happen is that one of us could fall into the water and possibly be swept away with the current—*if* there's a current. But the chances of that happening are, like, a gazillion to one."

"Uh-huh," Jules responded, offering me his arm as we made our descent down the steps. He popped his own mint into his mouth and shoved the empty wrapper into his pants pocket. "And you wonder why I've been tutoring you a little extra for this exam tomorrow. You *do* know that the statistic you just made up is outrageous, right?"

I quickly grabbed his arm and matched his pace as we took one step at a time. "The second worst thing would be that we'd get caught and possibly arrested," I said, ignoring his question. "But we're too cool for that."

"Seriously, Alex, I don't think this is a good idea. I've noticed that lately you've become less cautious with the smaller things in life, and that's great. But *this* isn't something you toss caution to the wind for. One of us could really get hurt." He gently grabbed my arm as I tried to walk around to the back of the restaurant when we got to the bottom of the steps.

"Come on, Jules. We can pretend we're pirates."

I slipped out of his light grip and began to jump and poke at him with an imaginary sword. He shook his head and looked around, wondering if other people were watching what was happening.

"I haven't played pirates since I was a kid," Jules groaned.

"All the more reason to check it out. I bet it won't take long," I challenged. "If there's nothing in there, then we'll leave. But if we *find* something, then we'll split the findings fifty-fifty." I stood up straight from my fencing pose and extended an open hand to him. He looked at it for a few seconds and thought about it. I knew my Cheshire grin was hard to ignore.

He exhaled loudly but couldn't help smiling as well. "To date, you're the most ridiculous person I know."

"More ridiculous than James?"

"That's a tough one to answer."

I stepped closer to him with my hand still open to seal the deal. "Come on. What say you? Be ridiculous *with* me. If something happens, good or bad, we'll both be in it together, regardless."

He still hesitated.

"Come on, you land-loving eel-eater. What do we have to lose?" I cooed.

He stared at me for a few more seconds, and then reluctantly placed his hand into mine.

"Great! Let's get moving, before the clouds block our only source of light!"

Chapter 24

After walking through soggy grass and around some garbage bins, we found ourselves standing in front of an old wooden dock that led to the ship. The sound of the water lapping the wooden poles that kept the dock suspended over the shore sounded eerie. Goose bumps ran down the back of my neck as I crept forward to get a closer look. The ship had looked different when I was eyeing it from inside the restaurant.

Jules grabbed my hand before I could step onto the rotted wood, pulling me back quickly.

"What's wrong?" I whispered.

"I *really* don't have a good feeling about this. We should leave." He released my hand and backed a few steps away from the dock.

"Don't chicken out on me now, Jax. Benny wouldn't be scared." I tried to reach for his hand to pull him toward me, but he put them both behind his back so I couldn't grab either of them.

"In case you forgot, we aren't pirates, and Benny isn't real. And *don't* call me Jax just to try and get me to cave in, *Marbles.* That won't work."

Jules didn't move an inch as he waited to see if I would go back to the parking lot with him. I knew he wanted to leave, and I wanted to respect his wishes. But I also wanted to see what was inside the ship. When I had my mind made up about something, nothing and no one could change it.

"I'm sorry, but curiosity is getting the best of me. If you're *that* scared, just wait here for me while I go. You can keep a lookout."

"I'm not scared. You *know* I'm not scared." He sounded as if I'd offended him.

"Okay, okay, you aren't scared. You'll keep a lookout, though, right?"

He sighed deeply in defeat. "Fine. I'll call you if someone comes around the back of the restaurant. Make sure your phone is on vibrate so the ringtones don't give either of us away." He reached into his pocket and pulled out his phone, changing the setting as he watched me approach the ship.

"Aye aye, captain." I said jokingly. I pulled out my phone and did the same, shoved it back into my pocket, and then looked over an old rope ladder. After a few light tugs to see if it was safe to put all my weight on it, I began to scale the side up to the deck. At the top, I climbed over the wooden railing and gazed around. With only the light from the moon, I tried to make out the items that were scattered all over the place.

"Some prop," I mumbled to myself. "It looks like there's real cargo on here and real docking ropes." I looked around some more and noticed that at the center of the deck there was an open wooden hatch that led down into the cargo hold.

Huzzah . . .

I walked to the small, square hole and looked down into it. A wooden ladder led into the darkness. I looked back to the railing I had climbed over, wishing that Jules was there with me so I wasn't alone. *I can't back out now*, I thought. *I need to finish what I started.* After a few seconds of collecting my thoughts, I bent over and began to climb down the ladder into the unknown.

Once I was below deck, I looked around at my surroundings, allowing my eyes to adjust to the dim lighting. Large black fishing nets were draped over shipping crates, and there were fishing lines sprawled everywhere. The smell of dead fish and mold crept up my nostrils and almost made me gag. I waved my hand back and forth quickly in front of my nose. Pulling out my cell phone, I realized that I had only been on the ship for five or six minutes. If I didn't find something in fifteen, I was out of there. I put the phone away, held my nostrils closed with my right hand, and began to walk around the back of the cargo hold, looking behind and inside every crate I found, while breathing quietly through my mouth.

I managed to look around the entire back part of the ship until I ended up in the middle again by the ladder that led back up to the deck. All I'd found were some crab cages, dirty buckets with nasty, moldy mops in them, and a box filled with fishing hooks and even more fishing nets. "Jules was right," I admitted to myself. "We should have just gone home. This was a complete waste of time."

I walked toward the front of the ship next to yet another wall lined with crates. "At least *he* won't smell like dead fish and mold." I placed my left hand on one of the crates and peeked around the corner to make sure I wouldn't trip over a crab cage again like I had earlier. I heard a loud creak as I put all of my weight down on one of the old wooden floorboards. Stopping dead in my tracks, I looked around to see if someone else was there, but came to the realization that the sound was coming from under me.

I didn't move a muscle, trying to control the fear that was starting to overwhelm me. I didn't want to pretend to be a pirate anymore. I wanted to get out of there. After taking a few deep breaths, I tried to step back to make my way toward the wooden ladder, only to fall through the floor. I caught hold of one of the fishing nets draped over a stack of crates that was just within reach, afraid of what I'd land on below if I lost my grip.

My phone suddenly started to vibrate in my pocket, startling me and causing me to yelp in fear. I carefully reached into my pocket, trying to keep myself from putting too much strain on the rotting net. As I fumbled to answer it, I lost hold of it, and watched as it fell into the hull of the ship.

"Oh, come on!"

I listened to it dance around in what I assumed was a shallow puddle of water. I could barely make out Jules's name as it flashed on the screen. As the vibrating slowed, the light emitting from it grew dim. Seeing as how I could *just* make out the name on the caller ID, I assumed that it was a pretty far fall from where I was to where the phone had landed. That was when I knew I was in serious trouble.

I tried to climb out of the hole for what felt like forever, before I stopped from exhaustion. The more I struggled, the looser became the crates the nets were wrapped around. I was afraid they'd all fall in on me, so that gave me another reason to stay put. Every few seconds, the floorboards above me creaked, threatening to break away more than they already had. While shifting my weight and trying to figure out what I should do, I heard more creaking coming from the center of the cargo hold. Seconds later, I heard footsteps. I was afraid to say anything, thinking it was someone that worked at the restaurant or even the police.

"Alex," someone whispered.

I waited to hear my name again.

"Alex, where are you?"

I was relieved when I recognized Jules's voice. "Over here." I called back quietly.

I heard him quickly make his way over to the hole when he figured out what happened.

"Don't come too close," I warned him. I shifted my weight again as the fishing net lowered a little more into the hole. "The floorboards are weak over here. I fell through some of them while I was looking around."

"Why didn't you call me?"

"I didn't think to. I was trying not to panic. I'm *still* trying not to panic. I dropped my phone when I went to answer it when you called."

"Okay, just hang on. I'll pull you back up."

I listened as he went to the back of the ship and rummaged around for something to pull me out with. After a few seconds he walked back toward the hole, getting as close as he could without endangering himself.

"I'm going to toss the end of a docking rope in to you. Let it settle, and then grab it, okay?"

"Okay."

The end of the rope landed in the hole and fell past me. I waited for it to stop swaying before trying to reach for it.

"Wait. Don't grab it just yet," Jules instructed. "Let me tie my end around something real quick."

I waited patiently as some of the floorboards near me creaked again, and the cargo net began to sink lower into the hull of the ship.

"Jules, the net won't hold me much longer," I groaned.

"The rope is secure now. Grab it and hang on. I'm going to pull you out."

"Are you sure you can?"

"Don't ask questions, Alexia. Just do it."

I worked my way over to the rope as carefully as I possibly could. My arms were sore from hanging there for so long, so I moved slowly. When I was able to reach it, I grabbed it and wrapped some of it around my arm, slowly letting go of the net and allowing the rope to hold all of my weight.

"Are you ready?"

"Yes."

The rope jerked, and I felt myself being pulled back up to the cargo hold. I didn't move, and I didn't speak. I just watched as the crates I was originally looking at before falling through the floorboards came into view again. Once I was close enough, I grabbed the edge of one of the larger floorboards and pulled myself up. I got one arm over the edge and held myself there, as he continued to pull to get me farther out of the hole. When I was halfway out, Jules dropped his end of the rope, and inched toward me with his hand extended to me.

"Don't Jules, you'll fall through."

"No, I won't."

I waited until he was close enough for me to carefully grab his hand with both of mine. He slowly began to pull me back toward the wooden ladder, where the floorboards weren't so weak. Once he was sure we were safe, he sat down next to me.

"Are you hurt?" he asked me.

"Not physically."

"This isn't the time to be a smart-ass, Alex."

"I know, I know. No, I'm not hurt. Just a little shaken up."

He looked me over to make sure I wasn't badly scratched or cut. There was a decent-sized scrape on my right knee from the initial fall, but it wasn't anything serious. He helped me to my feet and let me climb up the wooden ladder first. The moonlight was shining on both of us, as we slowly made our way to the side of the ship to disembark. He climbed down the rope ladder first and waited for me at the bottom, in case the pain in my knee got too bad for me to climb down all the way. He grabbed me by my waist when I was almost to the dock and placed me on my feet, so I didn't have to climb the rest of the way down.

We then trekked slowly back to his car. It was still early, but it was obvious that my side adventure had pretty much ruined the evening. He peeked around the side of the building to make sure that no one was there to see us coming from around the back. When he knew the coast was clear, we walked to the car as quickly as my knee allowed. He drove us to James's place before taking me home.

"I only have the basics when it comes to fixing scratches and scrapes," Jules said flatly. "James actually has a complete first aid kit. He'll clean your knee up so it doesn't get infected."

"You're not mad at me, are you?"

"No. But I *told* you someone would get hurt."

"I'm sorry. You were right. I was wrong. We should have left. It's just a scrape, though. It's not that serious. Don't make it sound like I was on a suicide mission or anything. I'm sure I wouldn't have died."

"Don't say that."

"What? That I wouldn't have died?"

"Yes."

"Okay. Can I say I wasn't going to get myself killed?"

"I just don't like the thought of it—or the topic, for that matter. So let's just drop it."

"If you insist."

One of the things I learned about Jules as I got to know him better was that there was a lot that seemed to put him on edge. Certain action movies that involved guns and high-speed chases, live coverage of random shootouts and police standoffs, certain noises while we were out that caused him to nearly jump out of his skin . . . it was weird. But I didn't ask about it. I just figured it was a personal quirk of his. If he'd wanted to discuss it with me, he would have.

After letting James clean up my knee, Jules took me home for the night. I apologized again for pretty much messing up the evening.

"Promise me you won't do anything like that again." Jules brushed some leftover cobweb out of my hair while we stood at the front door. "Keep it simple: climb the willow tree; try new food with me; stand up to Jordan—stuff like that."

"I promise."

"Good. I'll see you in class tomorrow. Make sure you keep that knee clean."

I watched as he got into his car and left. My parents were already asleep, so that was a plus. I wouldn't have to answer questions as to why I was so dirty—or explain why there was a hole in the knee of my jeans. After washing up and looking over a few algebra notes, I crawled into bed and tried to forget all the negatives that had happened that night.

Chapter 25

"Why'd you even let her get on that raggedy ship to begin with?"

James paced back and forth in front of me as I sat on the corner of his couch, staring blankly at the coffee table. I had gone back to his place after dropping Alex off for the night, so I could tell him what had happened that evening in detail and to release some steam. I'd told her I wasn't angry with her, but the truth was, I was thoroughly pissed.

"She insisted on going. I'm not sure where all this extra confidence came from, but she was dead set on climbing up there to see what was inside."

"She got this extra confidence because of *you*. It's because she feels *safe* when she's with you. That makes sense to you, doesn't it? Something about you makes her feel like she can do anything. But it's *got* to be used in moderation. Standing up to Jordan? That was a great way of using that extra confidence. Getting on that ship because she let her imagination get the best of her, though? That was just stupid. And *you* were stupid for letting her go up there alone, if at all. And why is she comparing you to Benny? Actually, who *is* Benny?"

"Don't worry about who that is." I tried to suppress a laugh. Hearing the name of her imaginary friend made me feel less angry.

"*None* of this is funny."

"I know. I just . . . I can't be mad when that name is brought up."

"What is it, some code word you two have for something I really don't want to know about?"

"Benny is someone Alex made up a few years back."

"Well t*hat's* not weird or anything," James said sarcastically. "Regardless, you need to keep her in line when you guys are out. I'm not saying to tell her what to do or anything, but she *can't* go around trying to be something or someone she's not. Part of the agreement when you came back to befriend her was that you were to look out for her too. You know, help her make reasonable decisions and to stay out of trouble."

"She was dead set on getting inside that ship, though!"

"Then you should have gone with her!" James shouted to get his point across, throwing his hands in the air as he flopped onto the couch. "You either follow through with her ridiculousness to keep her safe, or she doesn't go through with it at all. There's no, 'Hey, I've changed my mind. This isn't a good idea, so I'll hang back and let you wander off on your own.' You *know* getting that scrape on her knee wasn't the worst that could've happened to her."

"But the worst *didn't* happen."

"What if it *had*, Julian?"

"I'd rather not entertain the what-ifs or hypothetical situations, James."

"Then *don't* let her get ahead of herself like that again. I've never contemplated getting on that ship in all the years

I've known it was back there. Sure, I've imagined what'd be on there and what it'd be like to check it out, but I've never followed through with it."

After I ensured him that I understood and that something like that would never happen again, we talked about the other incident that had happened that night.

"The owner came out there just in time. What's his name again?"

"Tom."

"Yeah, Tom. He came out there just in time. I'm almost positive a fight was going to break out between me and Jordan. I'm not too sure what Alex was trying to do when she stepped between us as he advanced toward me, but it gave me a chance to decide which fist I was going to throw first, if it came down to it."

"Was tonight the first time you two have seen each other since the incident in the courtyard a few months ago?"

"Yeah. And apparently he didn't know Alora and I had a class together until tonight."

"Well, that's his problem. I didn't know he was so confrontational, though."

"That's what Alex said." I told him as I got up and made my way to the front door. I pulled my arms across my chest to stretch them out because they were sore from saving Alex from her failed treasure hunt.

"I wish I could have been there to straighten Jordan out myself." James yawned. "I'm just glad Tom stepped in to send him on his way. You've got that final exam for algebra tomorrow, right?"

I stepped out into the breezeway and stretched. "First thing in the morning."

"And then?"

"I'll be free the rest of the day. Alex has to work."

"Swing by the flea market afterward, then. You can shadow me at *Plates & Frames R Us*, and if you're interested in what you see, you can work with me. The manager already said it was okay to bring you on."

"Okay, good. Alex has been asking too many questions about my job hunt lately. She hasn't asked how I've been getting money, but I don't want her to start. Today, she suggested that I work with you, so going there tomorrow will be perfect timing."

"I'll see you tomorrow, then."

I sluggishly made my way down to my apartment. My arms were starting to get stiff from lugging the heavy docking rope from the back of the cargo hold of the ship to pull Alex out of the hole. Dragging her up and across the floorboards had been no easy task either. Once I was settled in bed, the overall exhaustion from the day's events pulled me into a deep sleep before I realized my eyes were closed.

"Jax!"

My eyes flew open when I heard someone shout my name. I was back inside the ship again, looking down into the hole I had pulled Alex out of. I looked over and saw the little girl in the white dress sitting on one of the crates on a pile of fishing nets.

"Were you here when this happened?"

She nodded as she slid off the crate and walked around the hole and over to me.

"I made sure she was able to grab something so she could stop herself from falling completely into the hull of the ship," she said quietly.

"Thank you."

"Just helping you help her. That's my job."

We gazed into the hole a little while longer. That's when I saw something glisten from inside of it.

"What was that?"

The little girl took my hand and pulled me down into the darkness. We slowly floated down from where we had been standing and landed on a small pile of broken floorboards. I assumed they were from the section that had broken beneath Alex. After my eyes adjusted so I could see a little better, I looked around, and saw multiple, vertical poles—wooden and metal—jutting through the keel of the ship. They looked very sharp at the tips. Alex's broken cell phone was among them. It was like a death trap from an adventure movie. I figured the poles were there to secure the ship and keep it from washing off the shore. I then came to the realization that if Alex hadn't grabbed the fishing nets in time, she could have gotten badly hurt . . . or worse. The thought of it caused my head to spin, and I felt a little nauseated.

The little girl looked up at me and squeezed my hand. "I don't need to explain what *could* have happened, right?"

"James ran the what-if scenario past me already."

"Good."

She took us both back up into the cargo hold to the wooden ladder that led to the upper deck.

"I can only do so much to help you when it comes to helping her, Jax. Something of this nature *can't* happen again. I can't guarantee her safety, only yours—to a certain extent, of course."

"Did G send you to tell me this?"

"I'm here on my own accord. G prefers the stand-back-and-help-when-necessary approach."

"That makes sense."

We climbed up to the deck and sat on the wooden railing that looked out to the inlet. The water was still as glass, reflecting the moon and stars from above.

"You know, you've been helping me quite a bit, and I don't even know your name," I said, as I watched her play with a bright-red yo-yo over the edge of the ship.

"Marie."

"How old are you, Marie?"

"Nine." She wound the string of the yo-yo around the bright-red plastic and shoved it into one of her dress pockets as she kicked her legs out in front of her.

"For a nine-year-old, you're really mature," I complimented.

"Thanks. G told me the same thing. That's why I get assigned to people like you for a short time, in case you need a little help when it comes to your special task."

"You've never wanted to come back yourself?"

"Nope. Besides, I can't take care of myself on my own down here. It just doesn't work for someone my age."

"Well, what if you requested to come back as something else?"

"You mean, get reincarnated?"

"Sure."

"Hmm . . . I've never considered that as an option." She looked thoughtfully into the sky. "What would *you* come back as, if you had that choice?"

"Oh, I don't know. Something helpful or really cool. What about you?"

"I always had a thing for wolves when I was alive. I think that's what I'd come back as. I'm sure I could find a way to be helpful in that form."

"I'm sure you could." I smiled. "If you don't mind me asking, how'd you pass away?"

"I *do* mind. And I don't want to talk about it."

"Fair enough."

We talked for a little while longer as we watched the clouds drift slowly across the sky. Even though she didn't tell me how she'd passed away, she did talk to me about her family she had to leave behind. I talked to her about my family and friends as well, so the conversation wasn't one-sided. I wanted to ask her if she knew how my parents were doing, but I decided it was best for me not to know. It wasn't something I wanted to dwell on when I woke up the next morning.

The sky started to turn a light blue, signaling to me that it was time to wake up.

"It was good seeing you again, Marie," I said.

"It was good seeing you again too, Jax. Hopefully, when we meet again, it'll be under different circumstances."

She hugged me tightly around my waist as she started to fade away. The sound of my alarm on my cell phone pulled me out of my sleep. I found myself sitting straight up at the edge of the bed—the same way I'd been sitting on the wooden railing in my dream. My arms felt less sore than they had the night before, so that was a definite plus. After cutting off the alarm, I started getting ready for school. I looked forward to seeing what it would be like to work with James later that afternoon.

Chapter 26

My knee was a little sore from the accident the night before, but I knew with time it would heal. It wasn't easy for me to lie to my parents about why I needed to buy a new cell phone sometime that day, but they bought it.

"We've told you time and time again to not leave your stuff lying around for other people to get their hands on," my father lectured as I finished my breakfast. "Are you *sure* Julian doesn't have it?"

"I asked him when he dropped me off. He doesn't have it, so I'll just have to get a new one today while I'm on my lunch break or before I go to work."

"That won't set you back or anything?" My mother took away my empty glass and put the box of cereal away for me, since I was running a little late and wouldn't be able to do it myself.

"I really don't have time to discuss this right now. I've got to get to class. If I'm late, I won't be allowed to take the final."

When I pushed my chair away, I bumped my knee on the leg of the table. I winced, making sure not to yelp in pain. Neither of them noticed as they worked to tidy up the kitchen around me. I quickly went to my room to grab my work clothes, apron, and purse. My parents were waiting for me at the front door when I was about to leave for the day.

"When you get there, ask Julian if you can use his phone so you can call and let us know you arrived at school safely. I don't like that you don't have a phone. And make sure you call and let us know when you've gotten to work and when you've gotten a new phone." My mother brushed some lint off the shoulder of my sweater. It was getting cooler out, so it was nice to be able to wear some of my warmer clothes I had stashed away.

"I will."

"Have a good day. And ace that exam," my father pressed.

"I won't ace it, but I'll do my best to pass it," I said, laughing.

I met up with Jules in the parking lot so we could walk to class together. As soon as I saw him, I asked to use his phone so I could check in with my parents. I saved my home number in his contact list for him, in case he ever had to call them, and then gave it back when I was finished.

"I forgot that you lost yours last night. Do you need help buying another one?" he offered.

"No, I should be okay. I plan on getting one sometime after class—either before I get to work or during my lunch break. Probably not the same exact one, but I'll have one before the day is out."

"Okay. How's the knee?"

"It's a little stiff, but I'll live."

We finished taking the final exam, happy that it was the last algebra class of the fall semester. In a few weeks, we'd get our overall course grades online, so it was just a matter of waiting to see if I'd passed. We stood out in the courtyard for a few minutes to talk, since I had some time before I had to leave for work.

"Did your parents ask about your phone?" Jules zipped up his jacket as a brisk wind blew around us.

"Yeah. I told them it got stolen. It was easy for them to accept, because I have a bad habit of leaving my stuff around for other people to take."

"Did they notice you limping any?"

"Nah, I was able to play that off. Are we still on for the stick shift lesson tomorrow?"

"That depends."

"On?" I raised an eyebrow, awaiting his answer.

"I'm going to *Plates & Frames R Us* today to shadow James while he's working. If I like the job enough, his manager said I can work there with him. I can't see why I wouldn't accept the position, so I'll probably start tomorrow."

"Oh."

I had been looking forward to learning something new from him, but I was happy that he'd been able to find a job—especially since it would be with someone he enjoyed spending time with, other than me. I was starting to wonder where he was getting the money to pay for his rent and all the outings we'd been going on since we met, but I hadn't asked, because I figured it wasn't any of my business.

"Don't look so disappointed. We'll have all of winter break. I'm not going anywhere."

"You'd better *not*." I laughed.

"Alex?"

We both turned to find Alora standing close by. She approached us cautiously as if we'd pounce on her, like a hungry lion would a gazelle. We stared blankly at her. When it started to get too awkward, Jules broke the silence by clearing his throat, and excused himself.

"I should get going. The booth manager will be looking for me in a few, so I should get there before he starts to think I backed out."

"I'll call you when I get to work and get a new phone."

"Call your parents first; then call me," he insisted.

"Okay. Talk to you later."

He waved to both of us as he walked away. I waited until he was out of sight before speaking to Alora. She was still standing there with a nervous smile on her face.

"You've got some nerve . . ."

"You know I can't control what Jordan says or does, Alex. You *know* I can't!"

"Why are you always making excuses for him? You've been doing that since week three of dating him. I'm *so* tired of it! Forget failing at standing up for your friend last night; you couldn't even stand up for *yourself.* What's wrong with you?"

She opened her mouth to say something but thought about it and looked at the ground.

"This is a joke, right? Why did you even bother coming over here to talk to me if you have nothing to say? If your goal was to get Julian to leave, you obviously succeeded."

"That wasn't what I was trying to do."

"Then what is it that you want, Alora? Spit it out already, before your handler shows up and you can't get a word in edgewise."

No sooner had I said that, than I noticed Jordan coming toward us from across the courtyard. I felt immediate relief when I also noticed Matt and Sam a few feet behind him, coming in the same direction.

"I just wanted to apologize for last night," Alora whispered when she noticed that Jordan was approaching as well.

"What're you whispering for? You shouldn't be ashamed of apologizing for anything, especially when you aren't the one who should be apologizing. *He* should apologize." I pointed at Jordan as he walked up to us and stood next to her. Matt and Sam slowed their pace and looked on, without getting any closer, when they saw the three of us standing in the middle of the courtyard.

"And I'm apologizing for . . . what?" Jordan put his arm around Alora and smirked.

"You should be apologizing for your horrible display of manners last night at the restaurant."

"Says who?"

"Listen, you can apologize or not apologize. It doesn't matter to me either way. I'm tired of *Alora* apologizing for your poor sense of social etiquette, when obviously you couldn't care less how you treat people when you're out in the streets."

"You're right. I honestly couldn't care less. I don't care what you or anyone else thinks. I can do what I want, when I want, where I want."

"Where'd you get *that* sense of entitlement?" Matt cut into the conversation, as he and Sam approached, taking places on either side of me to face Alora and Jordan. I was glad they hadn't left me there to fend for myself in what was going to end up being a verbal battle of epic proportions.

"And what's happened to you, Alora?" Matt asked. "It's like you've lost your sense of reality."

"Nothing has happened to her," Jordan answered.

"He was asking Alora, not you," Sam jumped in.

Alora didn't answer. Instead, she looked like she was on the verge of crying. I wanted her to say something, *anything*, to show us that the old Alora was still there. It wasn't like her to be so passive.

"You know, we'd have no issues with getting to know you, if you didn't monopolize all her time, Jordan," Matt offered. "We've wanted to get to know you for the longest time. But once you two started spending more time together, you pretty much took her away from us and didn't give us a chance."

"I don't need more friends," Jordan laughed.

"I don't remember you ever having many friends," Sam pointed out. "I vaguely remember you from high school, but I do remember that you had one or two friends back then. Then, all of a sudden, you took interest in Alora, and you dropped them and pretty much shut them out. If she's your *only* friend, you aren't treating her like one."

"I treat her just fine. She gets anything and everything she wants and needs, as long as she behaves."

"*Behaves*?" I shouted. "What does that even mean? How is someone supposed to 'behave' when you're dating them? Does she have to walk around like a mindless drone, not showing any emotion or sticking up for herself when you're more of a bully than a boyfriend?"

"Pull back a little, Alex," Sam suggested.

"Pull back? I'm *just* getting started! Do you only do these things for her to keep her around? Honestly, you treat her more like she's your property, just because you buy her things and take her to see the occasional movie a few times a week."

"Alex—" Matt tried to cut in.

"Let me finish! Jordan, you walk around here like you're all high and mighty, like you run things both on and off campus, when you *don't*. You're a human being just like the rest of us. Sure you may *make* a little more than us and *have* a little more than us, but you're *still* a human being—just like the rest of us. Bullying Julian the way you do when you don't even know him is low. Bullying Alora when you should be treating her like your equal is just as low. And keeping her from her friends is even *lower*.

"I remember you from high school. You used to be someone that everyone wanted to get to know. You were actually pretty cool back then. Then your parents came into a little money, gave you that job at the auto parts shop, and you changed into a different person. You're a perfect example of someone who lets a positive spike in their personal finances change who they are.

"And Alora, the four of us have known each other since kindergarten." I pointed to her, myself, Matt, and Sam. "You got mixed up with this guy and you forgot who your real friends are. You pretend like you don't see us on campus, and then you stand me up when *you* make plans to meet up somewhere. You've become a real flake. I don't like it. *We* don't like it. And if you don't do something about it, you're going to lose us. Unless that's what you want. *Is* that what you want? To be stuck with someone who *pretends* to be an amazing boyfriend but barely passes as an adequate friend?"

They both stared blankly at me, not saying a word.

"Dammit, Alora, that wasn't a rhetorical question! A yes or a no will suffice!"

"Alexia!"

Without realizing it, I had ended up toe-to-toe with Alora, waiting for her to answer me. She didn't flinch or take a step back. We were just looking into each other's eyes, waiting for the other to make a move. Sam grabbed my arm and pulled me back so I was standing between her and Matt again as I shook my head.

"Are we done here?" Jordan asked.

"Yeah. Have an *amazing* winter break," I huffed. I stormed off to my car, with Matt and Sam following close behind.

"You don't think you went too far, Alex?" Matt asked as they tried to keep up with me.

"I didn't say anything I haven't already been thinking or feeling for a while now."

"But you couldn't bring it down from a ten to a four?" Sam pointed out.

"I need the two of you to make up your minds. When you first met Jules a few months ago, you told me that whatever treatment either of them got from me was well deserved. Now I actually open my mouth to tell them how I really feel, and I should've had filters in place?"

When I got to my car, I tossed my purse onto the passenger seat.

"We did say that," Matt admitted, "but this caught us off guard. We didn't think you felt *this* strongly about how things were going with her."

"She's supposed to be my best friend. She ditched me, *us*, for *that*, back there. How am I supposed to feel? Like it's raining candy canes and gumdrops?"

"I get that you're upset about all this, but don't take it out on us," Sam said. "You're still amped up, so calm down." She gave me a hug and didn't let me go until I hugged her back. I could feel all the anger and frustration run from my head down to my feet. Suddenly, I felt a shooting pain in my knee when she'd accidentally bumped it with hers, and it almost buckled from under me. Sam looked at me suspiciously when she saw my face twist up from the pain.

"What's wrong?" she asked.

"Nothing."

"Don't lie to me Alexia Waters, you're hurt. What's wrong with your knee?"

Matt looked on silently as she gently patted around my right knee. I took a couple of steps back from her before she touched it again.

"You know, it's not something you can hide from Sam, Alex. Just tell her what happened." Matt stepped up next to Sam with a concerned look on his face.

"I don't have time. I have to go."

"You've got time to tell me right now what's wrong with your knee." Sam grabbed my arm as I tried to get into the car, and I pulled it away quickly.

"I *really* don't have time. I have to get a new phone before going to work, and I can't be late. Stop by the diner later, and I'll tell you what happened."

"Why do you need a new phone?" Matt inquired.

"That's part of the story I'll tell you later."

They stared blankly as I got into the car and got it started. I rolled the window down as they both approached.

"I'll see you two tonight at the diner?"

"Sure," they said simultaneously.

Once the car was warmed up, I pulled out of the parking lot and headed to the nearest cell phone dealer to buy a new phone. I figured I'd go there first and then I'd turn back to head to work.

I was almost to the small shopping center where the cell phone dealer was located. I was first in line, waiting patiently for the light to change so I could cross the intersection. While sitting there, I checked my wallet to make sure I had everything I needed to make a phone purchase. By that time, I was so busy deciding what phone I'd get that the altercation at the campus wasn't even on my mind. Neither was the pain in my knee. Out of nowhere, everything suddenly felt very surreal, but I wasn't sure why. When the light turned green, I pulled out into the intersection, only to have everything suddenly go black around me.

Chapter 27

I opened my eyes to find a white butterfly sitting on the tip of my nose. Clouds were passing by slowly in a powder-blue sky. There was sunlight but no sun that I could see. *Maybe it's behind me*, I thought. *Where am I?*

The butterfly flew away as I sat up slowly. My head was pounding and my body ached. I noticed that I was sitting near an unreasonably large willow tree in the middle of a green field. When I looked around some more, I realized that the sun was nowhere in sight, so I was confused. I tried to stand, but my body hurt too much to move my legs, so I slowly pulled myself toward the tree trunk and rested my back against it. As I sat, I worked to collect my thoughts. I still had no idea where I was or why I was sore all over. I remembered that I had left campus to head to the cell phone dealer to get a new phone, but I couldn't remember anything after the light had turned green.

"Hi, Marbles."

I looked up and found a little girl standing in front of me, holding a red rubber ball. She smiled and took a seat next to me on one of the large tree roots.

"Hello," I said to her.

I watched as she put her ball down next to me, and pulled out a small red bottle of bubbles from one of her dress pockets. She started to blow some into the air without a care in the world. After blowing a few, she offered me the bubble wand.

"Want to make some?"

"No, thank you."

She shrugged when I turned down her offer and continued to play with them. She looked to be nine years old. Her white dress shone brightly against the bark of the tree and the emerald-green grass. Out of nowhere, it felt like my head had just been hit with a wrecking ball. I shut my eyes tightly as I waited for the feeling to pass. To take my mind off the pain, I figured I'd make conversation with her.

"What's your name little girl?" I asked.

"My name isn't important right now."

"And why's that?"

"It just isn't. Do you know where you are or how you got here?"

I looked around again as the throbbing in my head began to subside. There was nothing around us except what seemed to be an infinite field of grass and the tree we were sitting under.

"I don't."

"Think about what you were doing before you found yourself here."

"Thinking hurts my head at the moment."

"I see."

The little girl rose to her feet as she tucked the bubbles bottle away into one of her dress pockets and then grabbed her ball and hugged it against her chest.

"Once your head stops hurting, it'll be easier for you to collect your thoughts."

"What if my head never stops hurting?"

"Trust me, it will."

She walked around the tree without saying another word. I assumed she was sitting on the other side to give me some time to myself. I still had no answers as to where I was, and I had no idea who *she* was. The second I tried to piece things together, my head started to throb again.

"Little girl!" I called. I waited a couple of seconds to see if she'd come back around to me, but I didn't hear anything. "Little girl!" I called louder, but she still didn't come back. I pulled myself around to the other side of the tree and discovered that she wasn't there anymore. I was alone again. *Maybe I'm dreaming*, I thought. *This* has *to be a dream.*

I closed my eyes and took a few deep breaths. I suddenly felt tired, so I didn't hesitate to leave them closed so I could drift off to sleep. *Hopefully when I wake up, everything will be back to normal.*

My eyes flew open to the sound of blaring sirens. I found myself standing in the middle of a chaotic intersection. Cars in all directions were at a standstill, crowds of people were standing on street corners, and the traffic lights were flashing red. The smell of burning rubber and plastic filled my nose, causing my eyes to water. Two ambulances and a fire truck were blocking my view from whatever was going on in the middle of the street. A few squad cars were scattered here and there as well. Curious, I slowly approached the cause of the commotion.

When I peered around the side of one of the ambulances, I saw two vehicles wrapped around each other. One of them was a company truck that looked like it was carrying metal pipes in the back or on the roof. They were scattered all over the road, while a couple of them were sticking out the side of the second vehicle, a smaller car. The driver's side of the car was completely peeled away like a sardine can, and the large piece of equipment that had caused that damage was resting on the ground. The car was so destroyed that all I could make out was the color of it.

Paramedics and police officers were standing around, taking statements and talking to the driver of the truck. He was holding a patch of gauze over his right eyebrow as he spoke frantically, while an officer tried to give him what looked to be a Breathalyzer test. One of the ambulances sped away toward the nearest hospital in town, leaving the other behind for the truck driver.

I heard frantic voices all around me. I saw a large group of students I recognized from campus, standing and staring at what was going on, with their mouths covered as they talked on their cell phones. A few feet away, an officer was speaking to students sitting on the curb. I walked closer to them and discovered that it was Matt and Sam. Standing behind them was Alora. Jordan was nowhere in sight.

As I got closer, I could hear Sam sobbing, while Matt tried to talk to the officer as calmly as he could. Alora was showing no expression on her face whatsoever.

"Alora, what happened?"

I stood by her and waited for her to answer, but she didn't even look at me. She was shaking slightly, and I could tell that it wasn't from the cool weather.

"Alora?"

I went to place my hand on her shoulder but I couldn't feel her. I tried to shove her, but nothing happened. I even went so far as trying to pull her messy ponytail, and *still* nothing happened.

"We've sent a car to her home address. Mr. and Mrs. Waters will be on their way to the hospital shortly. Is there anyone else we need to get in contact with?"

Matt and Sam looked at each other and shook their heads. "We called her job and let them know what happened," Matt managed to get out. "Jules is probably already at the hospital; I called him as soon as we found out she was in an accident."

"What's his full name?"

"Julian Reed, sir."

"And his relationship to the victim?" The officer tried to be as sympathetic as possible, while trying to quickly get answers from them.

"I know they weren't related. Uh, they weren't dating, were they, Sam?"

"I don't think so. Alora?"

"You two would know better than me. I talked to Julian in class, but we never talked about him or Alex. The conversation was always focused on me." Alora fought back a sob, covering her mouth with both of her hands.

"Since he's probably already there, we'll call the hospital and tell the front desk that he's her significant other," the officer decided. "That'll allow him to receive limited status updates about her until her parents arrive."

Victim? I staggered backward, not believing what I was hearing. I realized then that *this* was how I had ended up in the green field with the little girl. Everything had gone black around me, because I had been hit by the truck carrying the metal pipes when I pulled into the intersection after the light had turned green. The collision must have been so severe that I'd felt nothing. I ran back to the scene of the accident and learned that the large piece of equipment sitting by my car was the Jaws of Life. That was how the entire left side of my car had gotten peeled away from the frame. I saw two halves of the pipes still in the car door. The other halves weren't in the car, and neither was I.

Out of nowhere, it felt like my chest was being ripped in half. My knees buckled from under me, and I fell to the ground. I tried to breathe, but it was too painful. Another wave of pain went through my entire body, causing me to scream and close my eyes as tight as I could. "Make it *stop!*" I screamed at the top of my lungs.

The cold concrete disappeared from under me, to be replaced by a green linoleum floor, a bright light, and beeping machines. I looked up from the floor to find multiple pairs of legs near me in what looked to be dark blue and green scrubs. When I noticed that the pain had gone away, I quickly got to my feet and found myself standing among doctors and nurses. There were about five or six of them in the room, all of them silent and diligently working on something in the middle of the tight circle they formed.

I walked around them quietly and made my way to the center of things to see what was going on. I nearly fainted when I saw myself on an operating table with needles and tubes stuck in me. I watched as one of the doctors pulled a large piece of the same metal pipe I'd seen in my car door out the left side of my chest and then put a compress on it. Another doctor worked with a suction tool to keep the large hole that the pipe left behind dry. That way, any additional damage the pipe may have caused would be readily visible. A nurse was working quickly to remove shards of glass from my face and my hair, dabbing some kind of fluid on each gash where she'd removed the glass. Two other doctors were working on my left leg, carefully working around a pipe that was stuck in it.

"She's lucky the pipe didn't puncture a lung," one of the doctors said from under his face mask. "Now, if we could just remove the pipe in her leg without severing the artery, we'll be closer to getting her out of danger. How are her vitals?"

"Low but stable," one of the nurses reported.

"Has anyone arrived that knows her?"

"There are two young men in the waiting room. I believe one of them is her boyfriend, according to the officer who called to give him clearance to receive her current status. Her parents haven't arrived yet."

"Inform him that we took care of one of the major concerns, but we still have a lot to do to make sure she'll pull through. He doesn't need specific details, since he's not one of her legal guardians."

I watched as the nurse who was taking glass out my face exited the room after removing her surgical gown, gloves, and face mask. I quickly caught up to her in the hallway and followed her out to a small, quiet waiting room that was sunken into a wall. As we walked in, I saw Jules and James sitting next to each other. When they saw the nurse, they jumped to their feet and rushed up to her.

"Is she okay?" Jules asked.

"For now, yes. We were able to take care of one of the major concerns, but there's still a lot of work that has to be done to keep her stable. Have you heard from her parents?"

"They're still on their way," James reported. "They have a police escort, but they have to get through the traffic the accident caused."

"Please pass her status along to them when they arrive so they're up to speed. We'll let you know if anything changes." The nurse gave a sympathetic smile and left the room.

I watched as Jules balled his hands into fists. "This is my fault." He said through gritted teeth.

"You *know* none of this is your fault, Jules." James tried to calm him down as they returned to their chairs. "There was no way you could have prevented the accident from happening."

"If I hadn't let her climb onto that ship last night, she wouldn't have lost her phone. If she hadn't lost her phone, she would have gone straight to work. How is any of this *not* my fault?"

"Who's to say this wouldn't have happened on her way to work? What if she'd never gone on that ship last night but instead went to sit in the park for a while before going to work today? It still probably would have happened. You know this is how it works; you know this is totally out of anyone's control."

I sat next to Jules as he started to bounce his right knee from anxiousness. I could tell that James was trying his best to keep him calm, but James was on edge himself. I sat back in the chair when I started to feel light-headed, and the room got blurry. After a few seconds, I started having trouble breathing. *Something's not right . . .*

The three of us looked up when the same nurse came back into the waiting room. Her face was pale, and her forehead was drenched in sweat. She was speaking to both of them quickly. I saw a look of panic grow on their faces, but I couldn't hear what she was saying. White noise was filling my ears, and everything around me in the room was starting to smear and run together into messy shades and hues. I couldn't see anything clearly, and it felt like I was suffocating. Before everything faded away completely, I barely made out what Jules and James were saying to each other. The nurse quickly left so she could re-sterilize and go back into the operating room.

"I have to help her. This can't happen!" I heard Jules plead.

"You *know* that will compromise your situation," James warned.

I tried to hang on for as long as I could, slowing my breathing down to try to control the light-headedness.

What does he mean, he has to help me? What situation is James talking about?

"But it *can* be done, right? I can do it right here in the waiting room or in my car . . ." Jules's voice cracked from trying to keep from going hysterical.

"Yes, it can. You know what the consequences may be when G finds out, right?"

"I'll cross that bridge when I get there."

G?

James got up and ran to a nearby nursing station, coming back a few seconds later with two small white cups: one with two pills in it and the other filled with water.

"I told one of the nurses you were having a panic attack, so she gave me these. She said they'll help you calm down pretty quickly, so you'll definitely fall asleep in no time. I'll make sure no one disturbs you."

I watched as Jules popped the pills into his mouth without hesitation and drank the water. My eyes were starting to grow heavy as I still tried to listen to what they were saying. I couldn't hold on much longer.

"Make sure . . . find me . . . *swear* . . ." Jules was speaking, but his words were going in and out.

"I'll be sure . . . I swear . . . ," James responded, but his words were going in and out as well.

I watched as Jules finally stopped talking. His eyes grew heavy, and he slouched in the chair with his legs stretched out in front of him. James watched over him silently with a look of worry on his face. I finally shut my eyes and exhaled, letting the feeling of being light as a feather consume me.

~

"Marbles."

I slowly opened my eyes and found myself back under the willow tree in the field. The little girl was standing over me, still hugging her red ball against her chest.

"How are you feeling?"

"Tired. I want to go back to sleep."

"I wouldn't if I were you. If you do, you'll complete the transition and won't be able to leave this place." After placing her ball on the ground, she sat next to me and held my hand. "Do you know where you are or how you got here?"

"I was in a car accident . . . a bad one."

"That's right." She nodded.

"Am I . . . am I dead?"

"No. You're keeping death at bay; you're fighting it, but you're getting weak. I'm here to help you stay awake until someone else arrives."

"Someone else?"

She didn't answer as she peeked around the tree, quietly giggling to herself. I fought to keep my eyes open as she squeezed my hand, letting me know she was still there with me. I was too busy trying to fight off the need to fall into a deep sleep again to ask her what she was looking at.

"I saw two of my friends at the hospital," I said quietly.

"Tell me about them," she coaxed.

"James is this *really* cool guy I met through Jules a few months ago. Jules . . . Jules is my best friend. He got me over my fear of heights and climbing trees alone. He's helped me with a *lot* of things."

"Tell me more about him, Marbles."

"Oh, he's just amazing. It's like he appeared out of thin air, just for me. I remember the first day I met him. I wanted him to go away, but I wanted him to stay." I smiled as I remembered how determined Jules had been to get me to talk to him that day. "I'm glad he stayed and that I didn't scare him off. I introduced him to two of my other friends, Matt and Samantha. They love him. My parent's simply adore him. I don't know if Alora likes him, but I can't see why she wouldn't. We won't even talk about Jordan." I laughed weakly.

I then remembered how sad both Jules and James were when I saw them in the waiting room, and how panicked they had become when the nurse talked to them a second time. I felt myself tear up.

"You know, I don't make friends easily. I was worried that Jules would disappear like other people have done in the past, but he actually stuck around. I'm glad for that. I hate knowing that he's hurting right now."

The little girl looked around the tree again, a smile forming on her face.

"Would you like to see him again?" she asked.

"I'd give *anything* to be able to see him again and know that he can see me, too. They had no idea I was in the waiting room with them, and that crushed me."

The little girl slowly got to her feet, taking her ball with her, and walked around the tree to the other side. I could hear her talking quietly, but I couldn't make out what she was saying. As my eyes began to close again, I heard someone clear his throat to get my attention. I looked up sleepily, as I tried to focus on the figure standing in front of me.

"Mind if I sit here?"

It only took me a few seconds to realize who it was.

Chapter 28

"I have to help her. This can't happen!" I pleaded to James, as I tried to stay calm.

"You *know* that will compromise your situation," James warned.

I looked around frantically as I tried to think of some other way, but there *was* no other way. The nurse had just told us that Alex had taken a turn for the worse when they'd removed the severed pipe from her leg and that they'd almost lost her. I knew she was fighting, but she was also growing weak. She needed help. She needed *me.* And the only way I could think to help her was to reach out to her the same way I had reached out to G and Marie when I was asleep. And to me, logically, if that method worked to get in touch with them, it could work to get to Alex.

"But it *can* be done, right? I can do it right here in the waiting room or in my car . . ." My voice cracked as I tried to keep myself from going hysterical. I was desperate, and James could see that.

"Yes, it can. You know what the consequences may be when G finds out, right?"

"I'll cross that bridge when I get there."

Without wasting any more time, James got up and ran to a nearby nursing station, coming back a few seconds later with two small white cups: one with two pills in it and the other filled with water. He handed them to me and sat back down.

"I told one of the nurses you were having a panic attack, so she gave me these. She said they'll help you calm down pretty quickly, so you'll definitely fall asleep in no time. I'll make sure no one disturbs you."

I popped the pills into my mouth without hesitation and drank the water. After taking a couple of deep breaths, I could feel the pills taking affect. I looked to James dreamily and tried to collect my thoughts before falling to sleep.

"Make sure you tell Alex's parents what's going on with her when they get here. If they ask who you are, tell them you're with me. If it seems as though it's taking me a while to come back around, come and find me. *Swear* to me that you'll come and find me." My speech started to slur as I grew more tired by the second.

"I'll be sure to tell her parents everything," James said, "and if you don't come to in a few hours, I swear, I'll come find you. You have my word."

My eyes grew heavy as I slouched in the chair with my legs stretched out in front of me. James watched over me silently with a look of worry on his face. Everything around me began to fade, as I started to feel like I was floating. I thought about the call I'd received from Matt, telling me about the accident. I thought about how quickly James and I had left the flea market after I told him, taking the back roads he knew to get to the hospital as fast as we could. I thought about how guilty I felt about the accident and how scared I'd gotten when the nurse came back and told us they'd almost lost Alex. *Please let this work . . .*

I opened my eyes when I felt a warm breeze blow across my face. I found myself lying on my back in a field of emerald-green grass. Clouds were slowly coasting by in a powder-blue sky. There was sunlight, but from what I could see, there was no sun. I sat up slowly and looked around to find that the field seemed infinite. There was nothing else in sight except an unreasonably large willow tree off in the distance. *This must be Alex's vision of paradise*, I thought. I quickly got to my feet and started running toward it. It felt like it was taking me forever to get to it, but as long as Alex was there, I didn't care how long it took me.

A blinding white light stopped me abruptly. Then a large orb appeared in front of me and wouldn't move. When I tried to step to the side, it moved to the side with me.

"G, please," I begged. "You can't do this. I didn't go back to be with Alexia just to have her taken away from me. I'll be right back where I started when I died, and that wasn't part of our agreement. I didn't give up being able to watch over my parents just to lose her!"

"You know these situations are out of anyone's control," G said calmly. "Just as your situation was out of your hands, this situation is out of hers."

"But it's not out of *yours!*" I shouted. "I get that *I* didn't have a choice. There was no gasping for air or fighting for my life. But she's fighting for hers, just like James fought for his. You let him go back without completely transitioning, so why not let her? If she ends up coming here by choice, I want to be here when she does; you can at *least* give me that. But I'm begging you, let me help her. Let me help her hang on so she can go back. I'm not asking for anything but for you to let me keep the person I worked *so* hard to get to know and ended up caring about."

G didn't say anything.

"Please, *please,* don't let her slip away from me." I dropped to my knees in the soft grass and dug my fingers into the dirt. "I know you said that if she finds out about my true origin and purpose, I'll have to come back to this world and leave her behind. But this isn't fair. I get that life isn't fair, but this just isn't fair. If I can help her, please let me go back with her. And if I *can't* help her, let me stay here with her. Don't take her away from me just because someone was too careless to watch where they were going out in the street. We need each other, and her friends and parents need her, whether she knows it or not."

I stared at the ground as I waited for G to say something.

"I will allow this, Julian. If you can help her, you may go back with her. But if you cannot, you both will spend eternity here. Either way, you will still have each other."

I couldn't believe what I had just heard. I continued to stare at the ground, waiting for a "but" to be thrown into the agreement.

"The longer you sit here, the less time you have to help her. Marie is with her as we speak, trying to help the best she can," G informed me. The orb began to fade away slowly, as I brushed my hands off and got back to my feet.

"Thank you. Thank you!"

I sprinted toward the willow, full-speed, not realizing that I was holding my breath a good portion of the way. The closer I got to it, the more anxious and excited I became. I saw a small body peek around the tree, giggle, and then disappear. That was when I heard Marie talking from the other side of the tree as I slowed to a trot.

"Tell me more about him, Marbles."

"Oh, he's just amazing. It's like he appeared out of thin air, just for me. I remember the first day I met him. I wanted him to go away, but I wanted him to stay. I'm glad he stayed and that I didn't scare him off."

I suppressed a laugh as I recalled the first day we'd met. I had been so scared to talk to her. But I had remembered how much she needed me, which made my initial approach easier than I'd expected after only a few minutes of touch-and-go conversation. I saw Marie peeking around the side of the tree. When she noticed I was there, a smile formed on her face as she went back to Alex.

"Would you like to see him again?" I heard Marie ask.

"I'd give *anything* to be able to see him again and know that he can see me, too. They had no idea I was in the waiting room with them, and that crushed me."

She was in the waiting room with us? I hadn't felt anything out-of-the-norm while talking to James about how to help her. And James definitely didn't say he felt anyone in the room with us. Then again, his special sense only identified people who were living again, not people that were fighting to stay alive.

Marie approached me with a bright-red ball in her hands.

"Hello, Jax."

"Marie."

"You know, when I said I hoped we'd see each other again under different circumstances, I didn't expect this." She said quietly.

"How is she?"

"She's hanging in there. She's very tired, but she's hanging in there. I'm assuming you spoke with G?"

"On the way here, yes."

"So what happens when Marbles finds out about you?"

"If I can help her, I can go back with her. And if I can't—which isn't an option, but—if I *can't*, I get to stay here with her."

"I'm glad G accepted my proposition." Marie looked down at her ball and grinned.

"You two spoke before I arrived?"

"When I found Marbles sitting under the tree, I knew you'd come here for her. I also knew that your coming here would go against your original agreement. I left her here so I could renegotiate the terms and conditions of said agreement with G. We both knew that you had worked *so* hard to get to where you are with her, so there wasn't much to discuss. You two would be miserable without each other."

I gave Marie a huge hug, lifting her off the ground and causing her to drop her ball. It began to roll away after bouncing off one of the huge tree roots.

"Thank you so much, Marie."

"Anything for you, Jax. There *are* two conditions that maybe G didn't discuss with you before letting you be on your way."

"Which are?" I placed her back on her feet.

"If you're able to help her, your gift of being able to reach out to us this way will no longer be available to you. We'll always be here for you, but having dreams enabling you to travel to different locations and between the two worlds will stop. Also, she can *never* discuss any of this with anyone outside of you and James. If others find out an exception was made, it'll cause total chaos."

"Anything to keep her with me."

"I need your word, or else the new agreement is null and void."

"Marie, you have my word. I hate that I won't see you now and again anymore, but you have my word."

I extended my hand to her, and she shook it to bind the verbal agreement.

"Now, go do what you can to help her. Like I said, she's *very* tired. I did my best to keep her awake until you arrived. She has no idea you're here. Good luck."

Marie left me to retrieve her ball, which was now a good distance away from the tree. I brushed down my shirt as I walked around it to see Alex. She was sitting on the ground, and her eyes were starting to close. I cleared my throat before they closed all the way, causing her to look up at me sleepily.

"Mind if I sit here?"

At first she looked a little confused, but it only took her a few seconds to realize who I was. She smiled as I dropped down next to her and hugged her tightly. She hugged back weakly. Her skin felt cold to the touch.

"It's like the first day we met all over again," she said quietly. "What're you doing here? The little girl told me I was fighting off death. I saw you and James in the waiting room. I saw the scene of the accident and me being operated on at the hospital. Did I already ask what you're doing here?"

"You did." I got comfortable next to her, letting her rest her head on my shoulder. "I'm here to help you get through this."

"Are you really here, though? I don't understand how you could be."

"About that . . ."

She hung on to every word the best she could, as I briefly explained what had happened to me over a year ago. I told her how I'd been sent back to be the companion she had been asking for because of her strained relationship with Alora. I also told her about James and how he had played a huge role in helping me get adjusted to my new living situation. She only repeated a couple of questions, causing me to re-explain what I'd said, but I didn't mind. I wanted her to understand and hopefully retain what I was telling her—especially the fact that everything she was hearing had to be kept between the three of us: me, herself, and James.

"Your parents don't know about any of this?" Alex asked.

"No. And they can *never* know. Just like you were never supposed to know," I reiterated. "But here we are."

"Okay. Do Matt and Sam know?"

"No. And neither does Alora. Just James and others like me and him."

"And James went back for Alora? Does she know *that*?"

"She has no idea, so you can't talk to her about it. James isn't supposed to interact with her because he'd be an influence on her when it comes to her relationship with Jordan. That can't happen. Apparently, either Alora or Jordan has to end it before James can step in."

"Does that mean that under different circumstances, we probably wouldn't have been friends? Like, if this hadn't been a special task, you wouldn't have had anything to do with me otherwise?"

"It doesn't mean that at all," I reassured her. "If I had lived through my incident, or my incident had never happened, and I'd met you, we'd still be very close."

"Really?" She sounded surprised.

"Yes, really." I grinned. "Not everyone has personalities that mesh well together. Ours do; as do yours, Matt's, Sam's, Alora's, and James's. That's why we all get along so well. Maybe you and Alora don't get along too well right now, but I'm sure that'll change."

"I hope so."

She yawned and slumped over a little, not saying a word for a couple of seconds. I waited to see if maybe she just needed to take a break, but then I realized that she was slipping away. I shook her lightly, and she woke right back up.

"Stay with me, Alexia."

"But I'm so tired, Julian . . ." she said weakly.

"I *need* you to stay awake and keep fighting," I begged. "Do it for your parents and your friends—and for me."

"I'll try."

I got her to talk about everything that crossed her mind. I figured that the more she talked, the better she'd get. For every fond memory she spoke of, it played faintly in the sky above us. It was like we were watching a silent movie, and she was the narrator. After a while, her face didn't seem so pale, and her skin was starting to feel warm again.

"I remember that," she said as she watched herself run up to the willow tree in the park we frequented. "I had no idea that tree was there. I'd been going to that park for *years* and had never known. After I found it, I started to call it my secret spot. There was nothing really secret about it, since anyone could sit under it, but I liked knowing I could go there to have some quiet time to myself. Remember when we first climbed it together?"

"I do."

"We should do that again soon."

"We can do anything you want, when you're better."

The next image that came up was of her and Alora at the beach where Alora buried the lists and letters that James collected.

"Oh, I remember this too." She smiled. "We used to go there every weekend once we were old enough to drive. We'd just walk up and down the shore and talk. That was when she had time for me. I'd give anything to do that with her again."

"You can, if you just hold on a little while longer," I assured her.

"Jules."

I looked over and saw James slowly approaching us. Alex looked over as well and smiled.

"You came to help me too, James?"

"You could say that. Jules, you may not realize this, but you've been sleeping for a while now."

"What's a while?"

"I don't know . . . a few weeks?"

"Seriously? I thought you said you'd come after a few *hours*," I said in disbelief.

"I did, but I figured you would need some time. Plus, it took me a while to figure out how to get here, since, technically, going between worlds is *your* special ability, not mine. I found a loophole, though, with a little help."

"We're not still at the hospital, are we?"

"Of course not." James laughed. "I took you back to your place after Alex's parents arrived, because it was starting to look a little suspicious that you were sleeping through everything that was going on. A nurse helped me put you into a wheelchair so I could get you to my car, and the apartment manager helped me get you up to your place.

"What's her situation looking like?"

"They were able to stop her internal bleeding and prevent the artery in her leg from bleeding out, so she's okay now. They almost lost her again a few days after the surgery, but then her vitals started to become more stable, so I assumed you got here just in time. She's in a private recovery room now, and her parents have been there ever since. They're worried about you. They've seen everyone else come and visit her since we left the waiting room the day of the accident—except you.

"I can't leave her here alone just yet."

"I think I'm okay, Jules," Alex insisted.

"I don't know . . ."

"I can stay here while you go back," James offered. "If that's what you want, I can do that for you."

"I can't ask you to do that. This isn't your responsibility."

Before we could start going back and forth about who should stay with whom, Alex lifted her head off my shoulder, and slowly rose to her feet while keeping her back against the trunk of the tree. I watched as she fought to keep herself steady. James grabbed her by the arm to help her with her balance. Once she was standing straight up, she took some shaky steps toward one of the lower branches on the tree and then jumped up to grab it. She pulled herself up slowly until she was sitting on it and looking down at James and me. After taking a few deep breaths, she smiled down at us. I could see her eyes dancing as she swung her legs happily.

"I think I'm okay, Jules," she repeated.

"Well, that settles it," James agreed as he helped me to my feet.

A white butterfly fluttered from the branches above her and landed on her knee. Alex gazed at it, nodding as she started to hold a conversation with it that only she could hear.

"You can head back with James, Jules," she said. "I'll wait until you get to the hospital to make any movements."

"Movements?" I asked.

"James, when was the last time I opened my eyes or spoke?"

"When you were in your car before the accident, apparently," he said.

"Wow," Alex gasped. "That's a long time. I can wait until you get to the hospital to be with my parents before I show any signs that I'm okay. Anyway, I have to talk to someone first before I go anywhere."

"Who's the 'someone'?"

"What'd you say your name was again?" she whispered to the butterfly. "G. I have to talk to G first."

"Did you want me to help you out of the tree before we go?" I offered.

"Nah, I can get down on my own, if I have to."

"Come on, Jules. When we go back, you'll need to get some food in your stomach, since you've been out for so long. You'll be hungry and pretty thirsty, too." James grabbed my arm and started to pull me away from the tree.

"Okay," I said. I looked back to Alex as we started to walk away. "You're *sure* you'll be all right?"

Alex nodded. "Yes. I'll see you at the hospital."

We left her in the tree to talk with G, taking our time so I didn't feel disoriented or sick when I woke up.

"So?" James inquired.

"So?"

"You were able to convince G to let you come back, even though your situation was compromised?"

"I had a little help with that, but yes."

"Marie?"

I nodded. "Yeah, she played a big part in all of this. How'd you know?"

"She's the one who told me where I'd find you when I arrived. If she didn't approach me when I first got here, I wouldn't have known you and Alex were under that tree, and would have wandered around aimlessly looking for you. She also told me that she'd explain to G why I was here, so that was a huge help."

"Marie is *definitely* good at helping people; I can vouch for that."

We started to walk even slower as we both began sinking into the grass like it was quicksand. The sky started to turn a blinding white, as everything began to disappear around us. The grass tickled my eyes as we sank deeper into it, causing me to close them as we continued walking.

~

My stomach instantly felt like there was a cinderblock sitting right on top of it. My mouth was extremely dry, and my entire body ached. Opening my eyes, I realized that I was back in my apartment, lying on the couch. Someone was rummaging through the kitchen behind me.

"James?"

"Hang tight. I'm heating up some leftover food for you real quick."

I slowly stretched the length of the couch, listening to joints pop in my knees and elbows. I smelled horrible. It was a wonder that I wasn't skin and bone from sleeping for as long as I did.

"Here, let me help you."

James came around the couch and sat a large glass of ice water and two large plates of food on the table in front of me. After helping me sit up, he handed me the water. When I was able to get a good grip on it, he let go of it so I could drink.

"You smell like you've been sleeping with skunks." He laughed as he watched me drink the entire glass of water without stopping.

I caught my breath when I was finished and placed the glass on the table. "It's worth it." I took a couple pieces of ice and chewed on them, as I grabbed two of the three eggrolls off one of the plates.

"I know this isn't much, but it'll give you the jump start you need to freshen up so we can get to the hospital. This was some of the food I was ordering in while I stayed here with you." He took the third eggroll for himself.

"I swear, you think of everything." I grabbed the slice of pizza he'd heated up and tore into it, not caring if the cheese burned the roof of my mouth. Then I ate a few breadsticks and a couple of cookies. "You must have ordered in every night," I said with my mouth full. "I owe you big time."

"You're funny. You know you don't owe me a thing. Come on. Eat the rest of this and go take a shower. I have to run up to my place, so I'll be back down in a bit."

I ate the rest of the food on the plates, and drank the second glass of water that he'd placed on the table before he left. When I felt I was ready to stand up and walk around without getting dizzy, I took a long, hot shower and slowly got dressed. James got back just as I was pulling a thermal shirt over my head.

"Ready?" he asked as I walked past him into the kitchen.

"Let me grab something from the fridge real quick. Who's driving?"

"Me. You shouldn't drive just yet, since you've been asleep for so long. Give it a few days. Plus your car is still at the hospital, so we'll bring it back over here when you're okay to drive again."

After I grabbed a couple of apples and a bottle of water, we headed out the door. We took our time getting down the stairs. James walked in front of me, in case I got weak at any point and lost my footing. It was cold outside, and the sky was a weird, but beautiful, shade of gray. The grass crunched under our feet as we walked to his car. I finished one apple on the way down the stairs and was working on the second one as I got into the passenger seat. I started to feel even better as I finished off the bottle of water and chucked the apple core into a small empty bag James had in his car. We rode in silence as I looked out the window at the houses and shops. Something sparkled off to the side of the road and caught my eye when we stopped at the intersection where the accident had happened. I looked harder and realized that it was the license plate frame that James had made for Alex. Without saying anything, I got out the car while the light was still red.

"Jules!" James shouted.

I trotted across the street, without overexerting myself, and grabbed the scraped and bent frame from the gutter it was in after quickly shaking off the damp leaves it was covered in. I managed to get back to the car just as the light turned green, quickly shutting the door as James accelerated.

"Think it can be fixed?" I took a napkin from the glove compartment and dried some of the water off of it. The color of the cat's-eye marbles along the sides sparkled brightly as if they hadn't gone through hell and back.

"I don't think I can fix that. I *can* make a new one. Let's worry about that after we get you to the hospital to see her."

James dropped me off at the entrance to the building where Alex and her parents were. He didn't want to risk Alora possibly being there, so he said he'd be back later to visit. "Give me a call if you need anything while you're here. I'm shooting off to the flea market for a few hours." He handed me my cell phone through the passenger window.

"Thanks again, James. Along with Marie, you've really helped me through a lot of this."

"Aw, don't get all sentimental on me," he said, waving through the window. He pulled off as I walked into the building and approached the front counter. A small nurse was sitting behind it, filing away folders and charts.

"Can I have the room number for Alexia Waters, please?"

"What's your name, sir?"

"Julian Reed."

She quickly entered my name into the computer in front of her. "Ah, the family has been waiting for you for a while now. She's on the fourth floor, room 403."

"Thank you."

I grew excited as I rode the elevator up to the floor Alex was on. When I found the correct hallway for her room, I saw Alora sitting in the hallway in a stainless steel chair. She looked as though she was fighting to stay awake. I approached her slowly and placed my hand on her shoulder. When she looked up and saw it was me, she jumped up and hugged me around my neck. It caught me off guard, causing me to stagger backward a couple of steps.

"I'm so glad you're here! We've been wondering where you've been!"

She let me go and tidied her hair back into the ponytail it was in. There was something different about her. I couldn't put my finger on what it was, but I could hear it when she spoke.

"I've been coming here to visit her every day after class, hoping that maybe she woke up."

"Class?"

"Spring semester started about a week ago."

James hadn't been kidding when he said it had been a few weeks. It was a whole new year, and classes had already started back up again.

"Are her parents in the room with her?"

"Yes. They'll be so happy to see you, Julian."

"*Jules*," I said.

"What?"

"I've gotten to know you well enough to be okay with you calling me by my nickname. Call me Jules."

"Okay." She smiled. "They'll be so happy to see you, Jules."

I opened the door and walked in toward Alex's parents as Alora followed close behind. Alex's bed was by a window on the far side of the room. Her father was looking out of it at the parking lot, and her mother was sitting next to her on the other side of the bed. Her face lit up when she saw me walking in.

"Oh, Julian."

She got up, quickly walked up to me, and gave me a hug just as big as Alora's. Alex's father walked up to me and gave me a firm handshake.

"We got so worried about you when you didn't come to visit," Alex's mother wiped away a tear that was rolling down her right cheek. "Your friend said you were so distraught that you needed time to pull yourself together. He took you home a little after we arrived at the hospital." She rubbed my back as the four of us walked over to the bed.

"I wasn't sure if I could see her in any condition other than the one I'd left her in when I left campus that day. I feel horrible that this happened."

"It wasn't your fault, though, sweetheart. No one knew this was going to happen to her."

They both fell back as I walked up to the right side of the bed with Alora. I looked at Alex for the first time since the accident—outside of the world she'd gone to. Her left leg was in a cast, and there were a few small scars on her face, but other than that, she looked as though she was sleeping peacefully. I sat in the chair her mother had been sitting in when I'd first walked in.

"Has she said anything or moved since she's been in recovery?"

"At first, no," her father said. "But after they got her settled here and the swelling went down from the operation, and her vitals began to improve, she started to mumble a little here and there."

"Anything in particular?"

"It sounded like she was talking either to or about you," Alora said, standing next to me.

I took Alex's hand and held it tightly. It was warm to the touch.

"We've been waiting for you to come in, hoping that if she heard your voice, she'd open her eyes. We just want to know that she's out of the woods. We just want to know that she's still our Alexia." Her mother sobbed quietly.

I squeezed Alex's hand gently and scooted as close to the bed as I could, intertwining my fingers between hers. "Alex," I whispered.

Her parents and Alora watched in silence.

"Alexia," I whispered again.

We saw her eyes move behind her eyelids, as a small smile formed on her face. I felt her squeeze my hand back. Sunlight slowly began to pour into the room as the gray sky started to turn into a brilliant powder-blue. Alex's parents were right beside her now, holding her other hand, as they waited for her to open her eyes and speak.

Chapter 29

I watched Jules and James walk farther and farther away from the tree until they were no longer in sight. "I'm glad Jules came to help me. I don't think I would've made it if he hadn't." I slid off the tree branch and landed heavily on the ground. I was still a little weak, but the fall didn't affect me too much. Sitting on one of the tree roots, I watched as the butterfly landed on my knee again.

"How are you feeling?"

"A little tired, still, but not like when I first arrived."

"That is a good sign," G said.

"Thanks for letting Jules tell me everything about him and James. They did an amazing job at keeping that between themselves; I had no idea. I mean, I thought it was a bit odd that certain things bothered him and that he never spoke about his parents, but I didn't think much of it."

"He has a good heart," G said. "He was as lonely as you were when he was staying in his part of this world, so I felt as though you two would pair up nicely. He held up his end of the agreement and was willing to give up his second chance at life to stay with you. That was very admirable of him."

"It was."

We looked on as the little girl I'd met when I first arrived played with a red kite in the distance. The grass was so tall, compared to her height, that it was almost as if she were swimming in it as it swayed in the breeze.

"What is this place, anyway?"

"This is where you would have lived if you had completed the transition and crossed over. It's the one place you imagine that keeps you at peace when you think about it."

"So, this is my happy place, basically?"

"You can call it that, yes."

"Jules told me about where he was staying after he'd crossed over. It sounded really nice."

"It was similar to your vision of paradise but with a few more amenities."

I was growing anxious as I waited for some sign from Jules that I should start waking up. It felt like it was taking forever. "And once I leave here, I can't discuss *any* of this with anyone except Jules and James, right?"

"That is what he agreed to, yes. This particular situation is a first and will more than likely be the last. I would rather keep it so that others do not find out that an exception was made."

"I understand. I promise to keep this between just the three of us. Is there anything else I need to know?"

"Nothing outside of what you have already been told."

I looked up at the sky and watched as some of the clouds parted to show a faint moving picture. When it cleared up, I could see Jules, Alora, and my parents, standing around me in a small room. I felt someone grab my right hand and give it a squeeze, as their fingers intertwined with mine.

"Alex."

I heard Jules whisper my name from above, as I felt my hand being squeezed tighter.

"It is time, Alexia." G fluttered off my knee, daintily flying in front of me as I got to my feet. I slowly started to walk toward the picture in the sky. The little girl approached us and stood by my side.

"I'll walk with you until you go," she said, smiling.

"Are you coming too, G?" I asked.

"There are other matters I must attend to. You will be okay getting back without me. Always remember: no matter where you are, I will always be with you."

G began to slowly fade away. I waved until the butterfly was completely out of sight and let out a light yawn.

"Come on, Marbles. They're waiting for you."

We got to a place that felt like it could be the center of the field, and continued to look into the sky. The feeling of Jules holding my hand didn't fade as we walked. If anything, it felt more and more like he was walking next to me the entire time.

"Alexia."

I heard Jules whisper again from the sky and saw my parents and Alora get closer to me. The little girl tugged on the bottom of my shirt to get my attention. I looked down at her, as I started to feel light-headed.

"My name is Marie, by the way."

I stooped over to give her a hug and ended up sitting in the grass afterward. "It was very nice to meet you, Marie. Thank you for everything you've done. Hopefully, I'll see you again—under different circumstances, of course."

"That's the same thing I told Jax the night you climbed onto that ship behind the restaurant." She giggled.

"Is there any particular reason as to why you call us by our family nicknames?"

"I like the way they sound; especially when the names are said together: *Jax and Marbles.* It's got a ring to it, don't you think?"

I smiled as I closed my right hand, hoping that Jules felt it. "You're right, it definitely does." I said as I began sinking into the grass like it was quicksand. "*Will* I ever see you again, Marie?"

"Maybe. Only time will tell."

She backed away from me to give me room as I slowly fell backward into the grass. The ground began to disappear, and I closed my eyes as I was pulled down into what felt like nothingness.

~

Quiet beeping filled my ears, as the scent of cologne filled my nose. I felt extremely stiff, but I could feel people holding both of my hands now. I slowly opened my eyes to see Jules sitting to my right with Alora close by, while my parents were standing over me to my left. The sunlight pouring through the windows as I opened my eyes was blinding, causing me to scrunch up my face. Jules knew what was wrong right away.

"Alora," he said, nodding toward the windows.

She didn't hesitate to walk around the bed and quickly close the blinds, just enough so a little of the sunlight could still come into the room. Once she got them all, I was able to blink a few times and allow my eyes to focus.

"Alexia? Can you say anything?" my father asked.

"Say something, Alexia." My mother pushed the call button so a nurse could come in.

"She may need some water," Alora said excitedly. "I can go get her some water. Do you want me to get you some water?"

I nodded my head slightly. She left the room and came back with her arms full of plastic cups, a large pitcher of water, a small bucket of ice, and what looked to be five to seven small fruit cups. I had never noticed how good she was at balancing multiple items at one time. Anyone else would have dropped them all over the floor, including me. She worked quickly to get a cup of water ready for me, handing it to Jules when she was done.

"Oh, wait!" She flew out of the room again and came back with a long straw, ripping it out of the plastic wrapper. She dropped it in the cup with a smile on her face. "So you don't spill any," she added.

Jules brought the straw to my mouth so I could take a few sips. I took my time and drank. I had to take in at least half the cup of water before I felt more hydrated than when I'd first woken up. Jules smiled at me and gave the cup back to Alora when I was finished.

"How do you feel, Alexia?" My mother rubbed the back of my hand with her thumb as she held it.

I narrowed my eyes and swallowed, unsure of how I'd sound when I spoke.

"You two sound weird when you call me Alexia," I croaked as I tried to give them a crooked smile.

Both my parents laughed loudly and leaned over to give me the most gentle but strongest hug they could possibly give me. We heard the door to the room open, and a doctor and the small nurse approached us. I recognized the doctor from the operating room when I'd first arrived there after the accident.

"I see she's finally woken up," the doctor said.

My parents stood up and backed away to give him some room. He came over to me, shining a small flashlight in my eyes briefly. He then told me to follow his finger from side to side. I was able to do so for a couple of seconds, but then I closed my eyes when I felt a small headache developing.

"Something wrong?" the doctor asked.

"Headache," I managed to get out.

"We'll take care of that for you momentarily."

He proceeded to lightly stroke the end of his pen along each of my arms down to my palms, and he gave my sides a squeeze. I flinched when he touched the area where the pipe had gone through my chest. After checking the dressing that was over the wound while the nurse scribbled some notes, he then checked my left leg, which was in a cast. I hadn't noticed it was in one, until I saw him pull the blanket to the side to make sure it was still in place.

"Is it broken?" I asked.

"You have a minor leg fracture, and there is a large puncture wound in your upper thigh. It gave us a lot of problems once the severed pipe was removed, but it'll heal over time. We put you in a full leg cast, and wrapped your thigh in gauze as well to make sure the wound heals properly—until it's okay to remove the cast partially."

When he was sure that I had passed all of his sensory tests, he and the nurse took my parents out into the hallway so they could talk.

"We'll be right outside, Alexia," my mother said as she kissed my forehead.

"Do you want anything?" my father offered.

"Something for my headache—and for you two to *please* start calling me Marbles again." I chuckled.

"Okay, Marbles," they said simultaneously.

After they left the room, it was just the three of us remaining. Alora stood quietly and looked on as Jules and I talked.

"I'll never ask them why they call me Marbles again." I yawned.

"You know that I can never let you out of my sight, right?" Jules pointed out.

"I think you'll have to stand in line behind my parents." I struggled as I tried to sit up a little more in the bed, since my back was achy from lying at a small incline.

"I'll get it."

Alora went around to the side of the bed where my parents had been and elevated the back of it with the push of a button. I could tell that there was a lot she wanted to say, but she didn't know how to say it. That, or she didn't want to talk about it in front of Jules. She fluffed a few of my pillows and fixed my blanket for me as well.

"You're awfully fidgety," I said to her.

"I'm just glad you're okay." She held her hands together and twiddled her thumbs nervously. "Especially after everything that happened on campus that day, you know? I thought I'd never get to talk to you again after the accident."

"I'll step outside so you two can talk." Jules got out of his chair, kissed me on the forehead, and made his way out to the hallway with my parents and the doctor.

I waited to hear the door close behind him before saying anything. "Alora," I began.

"No, I have some things that I want to say. You've said and done enough."

I closed my mouth and listened.

"I'm sorry for the way I've been acting since I started dating Jordan. It was no one's fault but my own. I can't blame him for my actions. I'm more than capable of thinking and doing for myself. I just got *so* wrapped up in trying to make him happy that I put you guys and myself at the very bottom of the priority pile. Everything you said to me that morning was right, and I feel so *horrible* for the way I've been treating you, Matt, and Sam. You guys have been there for me through everything, and I shut you all out over one person. I've missed the three of you so much. I've missed *you* so much. You're my best friend."

I felt something strange when I noticed she was fighting back tears. It was something I had never experienced before. I'd always felt that I was an empathetic person, but this was something ten times greater than that. I remembered that, awhile back, I had never been able to tell if her apologies or pleas were genuine or false. Now, I could feel that she was being as honest as she could possibly be. She was emotionally naked, and I could sense that.

Without warning she leaned in and hugged me tightly. "I promise I'll be a much better friend than I have been lately. I'm going to work really hard to make everything up to you—from standing you up, to not standing up *for* you—everything! I'll do anything I can to help you recover and catch up with school, and whatever else you need—"

"Alora, you're hurting me."

She let me go and stood up as I tried to catch my breath. She had been squeezing me so hard, it felt like my ribs were going to break in half.

"I'm sorry." She sniffled as she wiped away some tears.

"What about Jordan?"

"Um, well, he's still Jordan." She said matter-of-factly. "He thinks I've been spending too much time here with you and not enough time with him. But I don't care. I've been coming here anyway, every day since the accident, until visiting hours were over."

"You know that Matt was being sincere when he said we wouldn't mind getting to know Jordan a little better."

"You know Jordan won't go for that."

"Yeah, you're right." I laughed.

I looked at her and started to tear up myself. I had my best friend back. Through terrible circumstances, sure, but I had her back. And it felt just as good as when Jules had come to help me get through my near-death experience.

"If you cry, Alex, I'll cry more." She wiped her face with the sleeve of her sweater. "I'll go get Jules. I'm sure he'll want to talk to you some more, since he hasn't seen you in a while."

She left my side and walked out into the hallway to get him. Moments later, he walked in, eating a banana and carrying two bottles of water and a large container of fruit salad.

"Someone's hungry." I stretched carefully and watched as he sat beside the bed, placing the bottles and container of fruit on the floor nearby.

"I didn't get to eat much of anything before heading over here."

"Where's James?" I whispered.

"He's coming by later to visit."

"How much later are we talking?"

"I'm sure it won't be an outrageous time—more than likely, a little after visiting hours are over, so he doesn't run into Alora accidently. We won't keep you up for too long, since you'll need to rest. They're thinking of letting you go home later next week so you can recuperate there."

"Thank goodness. I can't wait to be in the comfort of my own bed."

We talked for a few hours, giving my parents and Alora a chance to go home and rest. Matt and Sam stopped by after their classes were out for the day, with flowers and a stuffed bear in tow.

"We got Alora's message and snagged these first and then came straight here." Sam placed the flowers on a table nearby, while Matt handed me the plush, stuffed bear.

"We came to visit whenever we could," Matt said. "Our spring semester courses are a bit of a handful, but we've still been making time for you."

"You guys are the best." I gave the bear a squeeze and laid it next to me.

It started to get late. Sam and Matt went home just before visiting hours were over. Soon afterward, a nurse came in and gave me the pills I'd been waiting all day for to make the mild headache go away. I fell asleep in the middle of my conversation with Jules after taking them. The day had been overwhelming, and it was a huge relief to get some rest without worrying about waking up and not seeing Jules or my family and friends again.

Chapter 30

"I went by the one booth and grabbed these while I was there," said a voice. "The owner said you can pay in installments, since he'd heard what happened. You know the deal with the frame."

"Did you make it to the beach before coming here?" asked a second voice.

"I did. Thanks for the heads-up. This time she wrote a poem. I'll let you read it when you get the chance."

I slowly opened my eyes and saw two figures standing at the end of my bed in the dimly lit room. I started to panic. One of the figures heard the heart monitor speed up and looked over at me.

"She's awake," I heard one of them say.

Just as I was about to scream for help, they both walked toward the bed, and I recognized Jules and James.

"Whoa, hey, calm down. You okay?" James laughed.

"I think she forgot where she was for a second. I'll go grab her some water." Jules backtracked to the table where there was a fresh bucket of ice chips and a water pitcher. My heart stopped racing and the monitor began to slow down.

"I thought maybe I'd gone back," I whimpered.

"Oh, no, you're okay. You're stuck with us until you get called back. And that won't be for a *long* time." James pulled up a chair and sat to my left. Jules came to my right, holding a cup of water.

"Think you can hold it yourself?"

"I'm still a little sore, but I'll try." Once I got a good grip around the cup, I held it myself, taking a few sips of water from the long plastic straw.

"You're looking *much* better. I wasn't too sure if you'd make it, to be honest. Your injuries were pretty bad." James leaned on the side of the bed and played with a piece of string hanging off the edge of the blanket.

"I wasn't sure I'd make it, either," I said. "But thanks to G, Marie, and Jules, I did. How'd you know about my condition and how I looked—if Alora was here just about every day with my parents?"

"I know the nurse that makes rounds to your room. He let me in after visiting hours so I could sit with you at night—after sitting with Jules during the day."

"I'm sorry about what happened to you," I said awkwardly. "You know . . . your near-death experience. That had to be rough."

"It was at first. But after recovering and meeting Jules a few months later, it got much easier to get over. I'm almost certain *your* near-death experience was worse than mine," he pointed out.

"Wait, if you've been practically babysitting us both around the clock for weeks, what have you been doing about your spring semester classes?"

"I spoke to the counselor for the three of us," James said. "We'll be allowed to make up everything during the summer semester, so you'll have time for physical therapy and things. You'll find that when we're caught in certain types of binds, we've got a little pull."

"I see."

Jules took the cup from me when I finished drinking from it. He then grabbed two plastic bags from the table the water pitcher was on and came back over to the right side of the bed.

"Alex, James worked really hard on this for you today. I know you don't have anything to put it on right now, but we figured when the time was right and you had a new car, you'd want a replacement one."

He dug into the larger bag and handed me a license plate frame that was almost identical to the one I'd had on my car. The only difference was that there was a small halo over the letter *a* in *Marbles*—just like the small halo over the *a* in *Jax* on his. I ran my finger over the brightly colored marbles and tried not to cry.

"I don't know what to say, James."

"Say you'll have a speedy recovery so we can start hanging out outside of this hospital. This place is starting to give me the creeps."

He took the frame from me and held it, looking over at Jules as he rummaged through a smaller bag he was holding. I looked over and watched as he pulled out two small boxes. One was silver, and one was gold.

"When I went to shadow James at his job on the day of your accident, I saw something in one of the nearby booths that I thought you'd like. They told me it'd take a while for it to come in, so I told them I'd place the order later that day after working for a bit. I forgot about them when I got the call from Matt about the accident, and I never got to put the order in myself. But James remembered and did it for me while I was with you. That being said . . ."

He handed me the small gold box and kept the silver one. I handled it carefully as I slowly took off the top. Inside was a medium-sized, gold charm of the letter *A*, hanging from a gold rope chain. I took it out by the chain and held it in front of me, letting the charm spin slowly in the dim light.

"I got a silver *J* charm and chain for myself. Mine is the same style as yours and everything, so they're like matchers but with different letters. It's a token of my appreciation and . . . well, you know . . ."

"To also show you he gives a great deal of a damn about you," James cut in.

Jules stood up and took the chain out of my hand so he could unclasp the ends. James helped me sit up so Jules could put it around my neck. It shone brightly against the white gown I was wearing. I played with it between my right index finger and thumb.

"It's beautiful, Jules."

"I'm glad you like it." He sat back down and worked to put his own necklace on.

The three of us sat and talked about things that we could only discuss with each other. The guys told me more about what had happened to them and how their lives had changed because of it. James shared his story about his near-death experience in depth, sparing no details. He also expressed his frustration with Alora's current situation. I agreed that it was better for him to stand back and watch how her relationship played out. It would only complicate things if she learned that someone was genuinely interested in her with Jordan still in the picture.

Jules opened up about his family and friends back in California. He told us how much he missed them, and how he had watched over them for an entire year before being sent back to help me. His story of his passing seemed to sadden him still. When I asked him if he thought the shooting was an accident, he agreed. But he said he had no regrets, because he'd gotten to meet some new and amazing people. He couldn't wait for us all to become a tight-knit group. He said it was something he had been thinking about for months, beginning the day after I first met James, and he met Matt and Sam. We also discussed the rare ability James had acquired when he came out of his coma.

"I'm still working on it," he said. "I can't tell one hundred percent of the time if someone has had a near-death experience or has completely transitioned and then come back, so I try to be very careful when approaching certain people who give off that kind of vibe."

"Can you tell with me?" I put my hand out so I could get another apple slice from Jules. He had run down to the cafeteria to grab some snacks after James said he was looking a little sick in the face.

"I can feel it strongly with you, since this is your first day back," James confirmed. "Jules was a bit harder to decipher when I first met him, but I already knew he was coming because G had told me."

"What about you Jules?" I asked.

"I did have the ability to go between worlds and travel in my dreams," he said, "but I had to surrender that in order to help you. I did feel a bit "off" just before I found out about your accident. And I felt something when you fell through the cargo hold on the ship. We think I might be a bit . . . um . . . what's it called again, James? We were talking about this the day of the accident before I got the call."

"We think he may be a little precognitive. We're not sure yet, though." James reached his hand out over the bed, and Jules gave him an apple slice. "He didn't necessarily *see* anything; he just felt that something was wrong. So far, it's only been in regards to you, so that could be a good thing for your future trouble-making adventures." He popped the apple slice into his mouth.

"How about we don't have any of those for a while?" Jules took a sip of juice from a small juice box. "She doesn't have nine lives, you know. And hopefully *that* ability wasn't taken away from me too. Only time will tell, I guess."

"Did you pick up anything special while you were away, Alex?" James asked. "None of us are told if we're getting a special gift. We just kind of feel it when it's happening."

I thought about how I had been able to feel Alora's emotions as if they were my own and about how I could tell that she was being honest when we talked earlier that day. But being overly empathetic couldn't be as special as being able to sense if someone had died once or was in trouble.

Movement from the far corner of the room caught my attention. I saw a small figure standing as still as a

316

mannequin. Seconds later, I watched as Marie walked out of the shadows with her hands in her dress pockets. She smiled and placed her right index finger over her mouth, signaling me not to say anything. I looked from her to both Jules and James and then back to her.

"Did you want more water?" Jules got up and walked right by Marie to the table where the water pitcher sat and poured me a cup.

"Pour me one too," James said. "I'd drink some of that juice you're drinking that you got from the cafeteria, but it's a little too sweet for me."

"You got it."

They can't see her?

"Keep this to yourself for now," Marie said. "It'll be useful in the future. You'll see."

"Well? Any heightened senses or anything?" Jules asked me as he handed us our cups of water and sat back down.

I looked at Marie as she started to slowly fade away, giggling as she waved at me.

"Not that I'm aware of." I smiled. "At least, not yet."

Epilogue

It felt like a huge weight had been lifted off my shoulders after I apologized to Alex when she woke up earlier that day. The fact that we had come so close to losing her over the last few weeks was still in the front of my mind. At the same time her parents left the hospital, I went home to freshen up and try to get some rest. Jules had showed up to visit with her for a while, so we'd wanted to give them some time alone.

I'd been suspicious about why he hadn't been there at all while she was recovering, but that didn't matter, now that Alex was awake. Her parents accepted his reason as to why he hadn't been there, so I didn't say anything to him about it. After I got home and took care of a few things, I tried to relax, but I was still amped up from the day's events. Hoping the sound of the ocean would help me relax, I took a quick trip to the beach I frequented during the week.

I parked alongside a small group of cars when I arrived. The sky started to change colors with the setting sun, and a light ocean breeze blew some sand around me. I glanced at the people setting up small bonfires, as I walked briskly to the spot where I always sat to look out at the water. Once I got there, I flopped down with an exhausted sigh and kicked off my shoes. I pushed my feet deep into the sand and watched it run between my toes as I wiggled them. It was just what I needed.

When I'd gotten home from the hospital—and before I left for the beach—I took the time to write something to bury in the sand. It was my usual ritual, something I'd started a year into dating Jordan. I wasn't totally happy with where I was in our relationship. Once I admitted that to myself, I started writing lists and letters about what I considered to be qualities of the perfect significant other. I wasn't sure what Jules was to Alex, but there was no mistaking that there was a strong sense of loyalty between them. After seeing that firsthand in the recovery room when Alex woke up, I realized it was a quality I yearned for that Jordan lacked.

I was in an amazing mood, because my best friend was alive, and because I'd written the list in the form of a poem that day. Proud of how it had turned out, I read it aloud to myself as I began to dig into the soft, cool sand. "'Steady Searching' by Alora Pebbles." I sighed dreamily.

Every day I'm steady searching,
Whether I'm at school, or out relaxing,
Hoping to find that special someone that will cause me to look no more.
With every day I get discouraged,
Heart becoming cold like the mother bear's porridge,
Because I can never find someone that seems right for me.
Oh, when will I find someone right for me?
Guess I'll keep steady searching.

A friendly and loving relationship is what I'm after,
With a guy who won't treat me like he's my master
And who won't leave me behind and tell me that he doesn't care.
To know that I'm wanted and needed,
With the occasional undivided attention because I need it,
I know there has to be someone out there that's just right for me.
Oh, where will I find that someone who's just right for me?
Guess I'll keep steady searching.

Someone who's close to being just like me,
Who will like me for who I am, not just what they see,
And will give me all of himself without any ifs, ands, or maybes.
One who will lavish me with hugs and kisses,
And will grant all my reasonable wishes,
Which is only to spend quality time with the one person I so very much
adore.
Oh, where will I find someone who I so very much adore?
Guess I'll keep steady searching.

I see him every night in my dreams,
And I keep his qualities in mind so that, by any means,
When I do find him I'll be able to point him out with no question.
With a smile that makes me melt and forget the world,
Because at that point I'll know I'm his one and only girl,
A guy who's loyal, street-smart, witty, and meshes well with my own
personality.
Oh, where would I find someone that even has a personality?
Guess I'll keep steady searching.

I paused and looked around, feeling as though I was being watched. After realizing that no one was paying me any attention, I continued to dig and finished reading the poem aloud.

One day, without knowing, we'll happen to meet,
And neither one of us will have to seek
For that special someone that we see in almost all our dreaming nights.
How I wish I would find you now,
But I wouldn't know where to find you, or how.
So we'll have to wait awhile for us to find each other and start to bond.
Oh, when will we finally meet each other so we can start to bond?
I guess that will be when I don't have to continue steady searching.